D.W. HITZ

www.FedowarPress.com

ISBN-13 (Digital): 978-1-956492-72-9
ISBN-13 (Paperback): 978-1-956492-73-6

Edited by Heather Ann Larson
Cover Art by Don Noble of Rooster Republic Press
Interior Design by D.W. Hitz

Also by D.W. Hitz

Judith's Prophecy (Big Sky Terror Book 1)
Judith's Blood (Big Sky Terror Book 2)
Judith's Fall (Big Sky Terror Book 3)
Gods are Born
Brady: A Novella
Bloodtooth
Our Trip Through Hell
Garrets Lodge
Food Court of the Damned
Black Creek Mystic

———————————

Stay up to date with D.W. by becoming a member at
patreon.com/dwhitz

Chapter One

IT WAS HAPPENING AGAIN.

It didn't matter how hard she fought it; they always came.

Every night.

Relentlessly.

Mandibles the size of human arms clacked together, and the noise was deafening. They gleamed in the moonlight, the only shine in a darkness that surrounded them in a drenching gloom, a tsunami of hunger, despair, and isolation.

The creature was the first one, but it wouldn't be the last. It was the tip of the spear, the leading edge of the army to follow, and the monstrous thing rushed toward Nikka, powered by the locomotion of four chitinous legs, each tipped with points that stabbed just as well as they walked. Its thorax was coated in armor so thick that no weapon Nikka could find would penetrate it. The creature was a nightmare of nightmares, and just like before, there was no beating it.

She ran, and the cold night air stung her face. She didn't remember it being winter, but the air was harsh and abrasive. It ate at her fingers and stung her feet through her shoes. The night bore freezing teeth of creeping bitterness, a burn that started as numbness then set in and boiled.

It shrieked in a high-pitched way that reminded her of the sound her father's saw made when he worked in the garage. It brought a deep sadness thinking of him, and instantly a spike of fear because she knew that sound. It was a call to the others.

She raced around the side of a brick building. She didn't know where she was, but she assumed it was somewhere in the industrial district near Colorado Avenue. Those buildings were old and large, and many of the warehouses were abandoned once they stopped stocking them with grain and sugar beets, after all that processing moved to Three Rivers. But the air was sweet, and the inside was huge as she rounded the corner and ducked into the building. The floor was covered in dust and the desiccated remains of old beets. She was right, but that didn't help her, not when the thing rounded the corner behind her and entered.

It stood at the loading door, nearly filling a gap the size of a semitruck's rear. It walked slowly as Nikka backed away, and the sound of rhythmic, thundering clatter converged behind it. It slurped as its mandibles opened then clacked shut. It crept, relishing her fear as she moved.

She had nowhere to go, and it knew it. It had chased her there before, a thousand times at least. It would end there once the others arrived.

Her teeth chattered, the noise reverberating up her jawline and into her ears nearly as loud as the great beast ahead. Her heart slammed against the wall of her chest. Her lungs cried for air so they could fuel the oncoming screams.

The ground rumbled. The brick walls shook and shed years of dust. The ceiling rattled, raining down chunks of steel and ripping shingles from a roof that hadn't been maintained in fifty years.

It was when the enormous bug-thing was inside that the swarm behind it flooded through the door.

They spread left and right. Some clamped onto the walls and crawled up toward the decaying ceiling. All of them were as big or bigger than the first. Some had more legs. Some dripped with blood. All of them stank of mold and trash. All of them moved closer as she struggled to put distance between her and them.

It was an enveloping swarm. They were too fast to run from. They were too strong and too heavy to fight.

Nikka screamed. It was the only thing she could do as they raised limbs the size of tree trunks and stabbed into her legs. She screamed louder as monsters gripped her arms with mandibles and bit, slicing the limbs cleanly as others yanked from the holes in her legs.

The pain was a flash, a burn, and then cold. And then nothing.

She screamed again, though this time it was in her darkened bedroom. Thank god, she was awake.

The sheets were damp in her grip as she spun and scanned the room. She knew there was nothing there, but those enormous bug faces were suspended in her mind and she had to look.

Dirty clothes littered the floor as well as the chair at her tiny desk. On the desk were her schoolbooks for her online classes—they were all available as ebooks, but the physical copies helped her to concentrate. This one was *Modern Economics*, opened to chapter four on a page about widgets. It was right where she left it when she could no longer focus and was forced to attempt a few hours of sleep. She had managed one.

She hated the feeling of sleeplessness. She hated the constant state of exhaustion and the clouds that never seemed to leave her brain. She hated knowing that any time she set her head down, no matter the intention, she was going to fall asleep. It had ruined her life for the past two years, and she had no reason to believe it was going to stop any time soon.

All thanks to that one day.

Nikka stretched and let her legs drop over the edge of the bed. She set her head in her hands knowing it was dangerous but feeling like her accelerated heartbeat would be enough to keep her eyes open for at least a few minutes.

It wasn't like she had asked to see those damn things. She just happened to be looking through her bedroom window, and there they were, giant bug monsters dragging her neighbor Sully from the ground and holding him up high. They yanked a girl around as well—Nikka thought it was another neighbor, but she wasn't sure. But she saw them as clear as day: giant fucking bug monsters. That was the day the dreams started, the day her life took a downhill turn, and it had never been the same since.

There was a knock at the bedroom door.

"You okay in there?" It was Rich, one of her two roommates and her coworker at the Country Kitchen, where they worked as servers.

"Yeah." Nikka wished she could say she was embarrassed, but frankly, those days had passed. She was too tired and too used to waking up screaming. It was just normal now, no matter how much she hated it. She was just thankful her roommates were kind enough not to complain. "Thanks, Rich."

She heard Rich's feet skim the carpet as he turned and left. She exhaled and stood, stretched again. "Coffee." That was what she needed if she was going to be awake again.

Nikka left her phone on the bedside table knowing no one was going to text her or tag her in a post. She didn't use social media for anything except keeping track of what her cousins in Chicago were up to; they were her only living family. She didn't have friends anymore—not except for Corra, but she wasn't really online or in town. They all abandoned her one by one when she couldn't stay awake in high school, woke up screaming in classes, and was mind-numbingly sorrowful when her parents were killed on a business trip to St. Louis the winter after it all began.

No one wants a friend like that. It's a downer.

Her only use for her phone was pure utility and to watch cat videos.

Those at least made her smile. She did see the time on it before she walked away, though: 11:46 p.m.

It was dark in the living room other than the television. Rich and Lynn, the other roommate and Rich's girlfriend, were on the couch watching one of those singing competition shows. A kid no older than twelve was on the screen singing some Taylor Swift song, sounding mostly good other than a few breaks in her voice at the highest pitches. They glanced over at Nikka. She waved and slinked toward the kitchen.

Nikka emptied the grounds from the coffee maker into the trash as she listened. She worked in the light from the stove hood, trying not to be more of a pest than she had to. She rinsed out the pot, filled up the water, started it, and rinsed out a mug, all in a daze. It was the never-ending cloud of sleep deprivation that was her life.

The kitchen was slim, a rectangle that let her see through a window below the cabinets and over the sink into the living room. She watched the kid sing as she waited for her coffee to brew. The chyron on the screen said her name was Sasha Nocatee, and her face had such a smile as she belted out those lyrics. It made Nikka more jealous than she was comfortable with. She didn't think she had been that happy in years, and she wanted that back so badly.

She remembered howling on the log ride at Silverwood with Mom. The amusement park in Idaho was the closest one and the place they started spending her birthday every year after she turned ten—every year until they died. She had taken turns going from ride to ride, one with Mom, one with Dad. They ate funnel cakes and cotton candy, so many sweets she wanted to puke—but she never did. And she smiled. She smiled so much she thought her face was going to fall off. She screamed so loudly she could only speak through whispers for days after.

She watched Sasha Nocatee sing, and she wanted to shake that child and tell her to enjoy every minute, to savor every thought and store that memory away as close to her heart as she could. Because she might not be that happy ever again.

But she couldn't.

All she could do was shake her head and fill her mug with bean juice, French vanilla creamer, and sugar and head back to her room.

She sat at her desk and pushed her books aside so she could get to her computer. She needed to finish her homework, but it was only Thursday and her next class wasn't until Monday, so there was time. She was about to open Netflix when she noticed a little red bubble on her email app.

Of all the friends Nikka had back in high school, before the trauma of whatever happened to Sully Richardson outside her window and before her parents' deaths, there was only one who still kept in touch: Corra Moss, who, thank god for her luck, no longer resided in Custer Falls. She was the only one who tried to keep in touch when Nikka was too broken to be around people and the only one to reach out when her mom and dad died. She was one of the few people in the world who made Nikka smile when she saw her name on an email's From label.

The subject line read *check this out*.

Nikka's eyebrows raised as she opened the email.

don't ask me what I was googling when I came across this because I'll never admit it out loud - you have to see it though. as soon as I read the first paragraph I thought of you.

There was a link. Without a second thought, Nikka clicked.

A site opened up with the name *Strange Tales of the Montana Mountains,* and the page was titled "The Witch of Black Creek."

That title sent a shiver down Nikka's back. She had heard the name Black Creek before, but she couldn't place from where. The feeling made her want to close the page and try for more sleep, but the thought of Corra persuaded her not to. Corra had thought of her. It wasn't something a lot of people did these days. She imagined Corra sitting beside her giving her the comfort and the push she needed, and she started reading.

Nestled in the back hills of Montana, in the hollows that rarely get visitors, hiding under the shadow of Mount Custer, is a small stream with the ominous name Black Creek. It's not much more than a few inches of water most of the year, swelling to the size of a stream for the few weeks in the spring when the mountain runoff is at its peak, but that doesn't stop one woman from visiting it every day. The legend calls her the Black Creek Witch, and according to eyewitness accounts, she is a master of soul-swapping, animal communion, and dreams.

The chills returned. "Dreams?" That had to have been why Corra sent this. Corra wasn't someone Nikka would have called an occultist—she liked horror movies and books and all but wasn't into paganism or astrology or any of that stuff. But she knew about Nikka's issues with dreams, that she had been struggling for years. Corra was the only one Nikka told that sometimes she wondered if being dead would be better than dealing with the nightly terrors.

She owed it to her friend to read on.

The website's story told of an old woman who was rumored to live in a shack in the woods by that creek. Supposedly, she was so old that she was around when Custer Lake was created by the dam, and when government officials tried to evict her so they could reclassify the area as a national forest, she cursed them. The curse was that they would die from nightmares if they didn't leave her alone.

Once Custer Falls National Forest was established and her land was no longer hers, those same government workers all died—except for one. Apparently, he was one of the sources the blogger had interviewed for the story. According to him, he made a deal to work for the old woman to have his nightmares taken away. He wouldn't explain what the work was, only that once he was done, the bad dreams never returned.

A black-and-white illustration at the bottom of the page showed a haggard old woman—very witch-like—between a stream and a shack. It was dark and ominous, and while Nikka wanted to laugh at the idea, she found her teeth clenching together. There was something about the old woman's eyes in the image that drew her in. It was like she was looking at the old lady and the old lady was staring back at her. The shine in her eyes, the locks of her gray hair, the folded wrinkles on her face, even the fraying edges of her stained white dress, all seemed to shimmer as if the moonlight was fading in and out behind varying layers of clouds.

"Yes." There was a whisper. A feeling like the light touch of a spider's legs crawled over Nikka's limbs.

Nikka backed away from the screen and stood, closing the laptop. She picked up a throw from the foot of the bed and wrapped it around herself as she eyed the sleeping computer. The room had gone cold, and the lights seemed incredibly dim. The only thing she found to be in focus was her desk, and her eyes didn't want to leave it. In fact, she felt an urge to open the computer back up and read the story again. It was like a hand was in her belly pulling her that way, begging her to learn more.

"No," she whispered to no one in particular. She sat on the bed.

What was Corra thinking, sending her that link? What did she think? That Nikka would go find this woman? She was probably dead from old age, and even if she wasn't, there was no way some random hundred-year-old wannabe shaman was going to fix her dreams.

Those shimmering eyes, that wavy hair, the wrinkly skin all hung in her mind no matter where she pointed her eyes.

Nikka couldn't go back to the computer. She took a book from her nightstand, an old paperback called *Off Season* she had picked up at the used bookstore downtown. The horror helped her to not think about her own fear. It could help her tonight.

She crawled under her covers and, below her bedside lamp, opened the book. She only managed a sentence before her lack of sleep dragged her under.

Mandibles clacked, and she turned and ran, only this time, she got the feeling someone was out there in the darkness of her dream, watching.

Chapter Two

NIKKA MADE IT THROUGH the night. She had the same dream three times, interspersed between periods of waking and reading and other dreams that started out fine and somehow transformed into nightmares with varying sizes of bug-men. It was seven when she finally forced herself from her bed and worked on her homework. It was ten when she started getting ready for work. She had the lunch shift today.

Lunch at the Country Kitchen was generally a casual affair, especially on weekdays. She didn't wear any makeup, didn't do anything to her hair other than pull it back into a ponytail and play with her bangs a little to make sure they were neat. She wore jeans—not too tight or they would put off the older diners—and the required blue shirt. She would get a fresh apron from the laundry when she got there.

Nikka spotted Rich in the living room as she poured her cup of coffee for the ride, her fifth so far that morning. "I thought you were working today?"

"Nah." He glanced over from the couch. "I was, but me and Lynn decided to do a staycation thing and take the weekend for ourselves. I traded with Jesse for two of his shifts next week."

"Oh." She poured in creamer and sugar and screwed the cap onto her mug. "So neither of you are working all weekend? That sounds nice."

But it really didn't. It sounded like a nightmare. It was bad enough tiptoeing around them after her wake-sleep-wake-sleep craziness most of the time, but that was when they were sleeping all night and gone for good parts of the day. This meant she would see them—and worse, they would see her—every time she roamed the house in laps to keep herself awake or spent an hour in the kitchen just to make a single cup of coffee, hoping to prolong any trip away from her room and, more importantly, her bed.

She would get through it. But she was not happy about it.

"Yeah." Rich nodded and smiled. "Just a nice, relaxing weekend."

Nikka hid her slow, accepting exhale and headed out to her car, a several-year-old Subaru she had purchased with some of her parents' life insurance benefits. Altogether, there had been about fifty thousand after she paid for her mom's and dad's funerals. After the car and the necessities to start her life on her own, she was down to a little less than twenty thousand in the bank. She knew a lot of people would have seen that as a fortune, but with no one in the world to look to for help or guidance and her entire life ahead of her, she refused to touch a cent of it unless there was an emergency.

She worked to pay her bills and her online classes. She didn't go out or drink or do much at all. Partially, that was to save money, but more than that, it was due to the nightmares. She had tried losing herself in whiskey a time or two, but it turned out badly. The dreams were somehow worse, and unlike while she was sober, if she had been drinking, she wasn't able to wake up from them. It was like they just went on and on, the fear without end, the pain in her dreams feeling real as those things ripped and tore into her.

So she wasn't much fun with others, either, not the kids her age, anyway, who liked to drink and party. It aided in the sadness. It pushed her harder each day toward the inevitable conclusion that this was not a life worth living, toward the understanding that if things didn't change for the better, eventually, she was going to have to end it.

She didn't know how long she had. It wasn't like she had set a date or started a countdown. All she knew was that her life couldn't go on like this forever.

That outcome was always in the back of her mind, though she kept it as far back there as she could. It was harder when she woke up screaming and sweaty, but she tried.

Nikka yawned as she turned onto 1st Avenue. The early spring sun was weak behind a layer of thin moving clouds. The subtle rise and fall of daylight over the road somehow reminded her of that image from the creepy website the night before, the movement of the light over that old woman's face. She imagined the witch's hair shifting as the breeze went by. From her occasional trips into the forest, she knew there was often a breeze that just blew all day, as if the air was having fun coming off the mountains and kept going and going, refusing to slow or take a break.

Horns blared.

Nikka's eyes shot open—had they been closed? Had she been asleep?

She was in the middle of the intersection of 1st and White Pine, running through a red light. A car was stopped on her right halfway through the intersection just shy of T-boning her. The driver, a middle-aged woman in a fairly large Chevy, was visibly pissed after slamming on her brakes.

All Nikka could do was cringe and keep moving while her heart pounded a thousand miles per hour.

She had been asleep at the wheel *again*. It could have been her last time if that woman hadn't been good with her brakes.

"Fuck!" she screamed as she exited the intersection. Then it occurred to her to scan for cops. She didn't have time for a ticket; she had to get to work. None ahead, she glanced in the mirror and went cold from head to toe. On the far corner of the intersection, watching her Subaru intently, was an old woman.

While Nikka hadn't seen the old woman from the story in real life, let alone in color, she knew in the blink of an eye it was her. The hair, the clothes, the hard expression in her eyes, there was no denying it—that was the Black Creek Witch. She stood, knowing Nikka was looking back and staring through the traffic, through the intersection, with a stance that made her seem hard like a statue while imposing like a wild animal. Her gaze shot through the mirror and chilled Nikka's insides.

Another horn.

Nikka jerked, focusing on the road ahead. She had drifted left and was barreling down the opposite lane with an old blue Suburban headed right at her. The driver was screaming inside his cab.

She yanked the wheel. The little Subaru jumped back into its lane, and the other driver laid on his horn as he passed and shouted obscenities behind his window.

Nikka shook all over. Her breath was tight in her lungs. She clenched the wheel, and her eyes moved frantically from the road to the vehicles ahead to the next light, everywhere another obstacle could emerge.

How could she have almost hit two cars? How was this drive going this badly?

She didn't want to do the next thing, but the wave of cold descending into her gut demanded it. She had to know. She glanced up at the rearview mirror.

The woman was gone, no longer on the corner.

She would have thought the relief would have instantly come, but it didn't. She was a trembling mess until she reached the restaurant. Amazingly, she was on time.

The coffeemaker was Nikka's first stop after clocking in. It was hot and as thick as mud. She didn't care. She wasn't allowed to use the flavored creamers—those were only for the customers. She didn't care about that either. She needed to be awake. She couldn't handle drifting off again. Not at work. Not if it meant she would see another hallucination of that old witch.

It had been a hallucination, after all. It had to have been. That woman wasn't real. She was just a picture on the Internet. If she had ever been real, it was like a hundred years ago, and she would have been long dead by now.

She gulped down the sludge, thinking the same thing she did every time she consumed coffee at work: *How the hell do customers drink this shit?*

Nikka barely had time to take another sip when Laurie, the hostess, dragged herself in front of Nikka and said in her grumbly, two-pack-a-day-for-thirty-years voice, "You're up. Table nine. Three top." She slipped away, back toward the entrance, and Nikka leaned around the corner of the beverage station to see.

Three elderly women sat at table nine. Their gray hairs were each shining and brushed to perfection. Their outfits were neat and pressed, clothes much too high class for the Country Kitchen. Nikka hoped they weren't the snooty I'm-better-than-you type that sometimes seemed to come in just to explore how the other half lived. But these ladies were smiling. That was a good sign.

She took a last sip of her joe and put it on the counter. She gripped her pad and set off for her customers. Dishes clinked at nearby tables. There was a murmur of voices from the kitchen. The dim light and familiar scents of comfort food and table cleaners fluttered past. All three pairs of eyes at table nine were on her as she neared.

"Where are you young ladies headed to all dolled up like that?" Nikka smiled and hoped the bags under her eyes weren't as large as they felt.

All three smiled back, lowering their menus. It was the one on the right of the round high top that answered in a cheerful tone. "It was picture day at The Heritage Club. We do it once a year for the photo wall in the front hall."

That made sense to Nikka. The Heritage Club was something of a private historical society that promoted the old days of Custer Falls, usually while skimming over the seedy parts of the town's past. She had never actually walked inside the place—she wasn't even sure if anyone under sixty was allowed in—but she had heard of the club suing places in town for doing renovations that changed the look of older buildings. These three appeared nice enough, though.

Nikka figured it was best to keep them happy, so she kissed a little ass. "Oh, I love what you guys do. Our history is so important."

All three nodded graciously, and she proceeded to take their drink orders: three coffees. She wondered if they would find the sludge as sickening as she did.

"Okay. I'll be right back with those." She maintained her shit-eating grin and went back to the drink station.

Nikka sipped her coffee and glanced back at the table. The ladies had set down their menus and were deep in conversation. She wondered what could have happened in the few seconds since she left to pull them so heavily into a discussion. She just hoped it wasn't about her. Either way, she wanted to keep them happy, so she immediately poured three mugs of coffee and set them on a tray with a caddy of sweeteners and a bowl of creamers.

As she walked back toward the table, though, something was off. The dining room looked completely different. The vibe had changed since she had glanced over just a minute ago. No longer were the ladies talking; now, they were each behind their menus, faces hidden from the restaurant. Strangely, that wasn't the only difference. The entire place seemed darker and colder, and the table ahead was the only thing in the room that was in focus. It was like she was walking through a haze, and that round plateau of seniors was the only clear thing in the building.

Nikka stood at the edge of the table and waited for a second. There was something about the situation, about the women, a strange sensation that she couldn't quite grasp. There was a smell of earthiness and a warmth that came from the group that pulled her closer, away from the chilling expanse that had taken over the restaurant. There was a feeling of closeness there, a kindred relationship she hadn't felt since Mom and Dad were alive. It made her think of those moments watching TV with them on the couch when she didn't care at all what was on the screen, only that they were there beside her. That was what she felt between these three, and at that moment, she wanted so badly to be a part of their circle.

Unfortunately, everything changed in the next second.

Nikka glanced down as she lifted the first coffee mug from the tray and set it on the table—she was working, after all, no matter what strange, likely exhaustion-based sensations she was having. But when the cup touched the surface, it was not the only thing on the table.

As she raised her hand, it brushed against something soft and cold and wet. It was black and white and red—was that blood? There were feathers and a beak, and a crimson puddle below the thing shined. It was a massacred magpie, and its insides were strewn about the puddle, over a pair of broken, misshapen wings and around its twitching feet. Its entrails stretched from its open mouth as if they had been methodically pulled out through its beak.

Nikka knew this couldn't be real. She had drifted off while walking. There was no way this could be happening. That fact didn't stop her heart from racing or her body from trembling. It didn't stop her stomach from lurching up inside her gut and her muscles from clenching in fear.

She raised her gaze, stepping back, but before her foot touched the ground, the lovely Heritage House ladies lowered their menus. They stared at her with glossy black eyes. Their skin, which had been wrinkled yet well cared for, hung from their faces like it was melting away. Their lips drooped, exposing brown teeth and widening jaws, and from each of their throats climbed newly hatched magpies. They reached out of the ladies' mouths and gripped their noses in their beaks. They climbed the Heritage women's faces, perched on the bridges of their noses, and started pecking at their eyes.

Nikka's foot never seemed to find the ground. It was lost in an endless void, and she was following it there, tipping backward into an abyss and screaming as she descended. She closed her eyes tight as it occurred to her those birds would seek her out and take them. The tray slid from her fingers, and her arms flailed as she fell and fell.

Then her back hit the floor. Coffee cups shattered on the Country Kitchen's hardwood. Coffee splashed and porcelain shards skidded away. The three elderly women looked down at her, their eyes huge and their mouths wide.

"Help her, someone!" the woman on the left shouted.

"Oh, Jesus." Laurie rushed over and kneeled.

Within just a few seconds, Ivan, the manager, crouched beside Nikka as well.

While Laurie was obviously concerned, Ivan wore a much more dour expression. He looked Nikka over and offered her a hand. She took it and he helped her up.

She was soaked with coffee.

"You okay?" he asked.

Nikka was so embarrassed all she could do was nod. She prayed she had only fallen and that all that screaming was inside her head and not out loud.

"Go on to the back and get cleaned up."

"I'm sorry," she told the table.

They stared at her as she turned and walked toward the kitchen.

Laurie picked up pieces of broken mugs and set them on the tray.

"Laurie, get a mop," Ivan said. He turned to the table and apologized.

Nikka didn't hear what Ivan told them, but she was pretty sure she knew what he was going to say when he joined her in his office.

Chapter Three

There was a thump as Nikka dropped into the driver's seat. She tossed her bag on the passenger side and shut the door, and as she turned the key in the ignition, the tears came.

It wasn't for her job. She liked the job okay, but waiting tables was tedious, even on the best of days. It wasn't the look on Ivan's face as he said that she was fired because, frankly, she understood his frustration. What grabbed hold of her and pulled her back into the pit of sadness she spent so much time in these days was the fact that she had no control. The lack of sleep, the constant nightmares, now these almost waking dreams... They were like a prison. She had been yanked from her regular life and incarcerated in this hell of impotence.

There was nothing she could have done to stop herself from slipping into that walking dream. There was nothing she could have done to change its outcome. She was like a passenger on a train that dove ever deeper into Hell, and she was trapped in the front row, watching it dive.

She hated this. Every bit of it. It was her life, and it had to end, one way or the other.

With the help of energy drinks and coffee, Nikka made it home and finished her weekend homework. Luckily, she hadn't run into Rich or

Lynn since getting to the apartment. She assumed they were having a bed party or something, but she hadn't looked for their cars when parking so she couldn't have said for sure. It was when she was in the kitchen, brewing another pot of coffee, that keys jingled in the front door and her roommates came in.

Lynn's eyes found her immediately. She looked away, trying to hide her disdain. Rich, on the other hand, actually looked somewhat compassionate when he saw Nikka. He came into the kitchen as Lynn headed to their room. The coffee pot gurgled as steaming water dripped over grounds.

"Heard Ivan the Great shit-canned you today." He leaned against the fridge.

"Yeah. They're already talking about it?" By *they*, Nikka meant Laurie, Jesse, David the busboy, and Yvonne, another server, together making up the usual Country Kitchen late-night drinking crew.

"If I was to guess, Laurie was texting me before you were out of the building. Wanna tell me about it?"

"Not really." Her voice was low, defeated.

He nodded. He squirmed as he stood there like a child, scared to ask his mother for a cookie.

Nikka sensed his unease. It made her a little frustrated—she was the one that got fired after all, but she figured she knew what he wanted to know. "Don't worry about the rent. I have enough in the bank to cover it."

"I wasn't." He shook his head, but part of his stress seemed lifted. Not all of it, though.

"So what else is bothering you?"

Rich glanced around the corner and down the hall toward his room. His shaggy brown hair swung with his head, and he squinted as he held back his words.

"Go ahead, man. I'm not fragile."

"Well, we're just worried about you." By *we*, Nikka was pretty sure he meant Lynn. "I mean—don't take this the wrong way—but you seem to be getting worse. You're up all the time. Now the job. I'm sure you can find another job, but if you can't stay awake at it…"

The coffee pot beeped. It was ready.

She didn't fill her mug. They just looked at each other as she thought about the near miss after running the red light that morning.

He was right. She was getting worse. But what was she supposed to do about it? She had seen all the doctors. She had tried their methods to desensitize and rationalize. She tried working out, positive imagery therapy, melatonin, lucid dreaming, winding down, bedtime snacks, sleep schedules, eliminating alcohol, rewriting her nightmare, having worry time, even a warm fucking cup of milk with a goddamn cinnamon stick. There was no cure for this bullshit. It was a chronic condition that was only getting worse, and it would continue to get worse until she fucking died.

"I know, Rich." Her exhaustion was about to bubble over into fury. She clenched her teeth and poured her coffee. "I know I have a problem, and believe me, I'm trying every day to find a solution." She poured in creamer. She added sugar. "I'll have the rent. The rest I'll figure out." She started back toward her room.

"Nikka, I just—"

She didn't stop to hear the rest. She shut the door and sat at her desk. Tears dripped into her coffee as she sipped it.

There was a stone path by the river, close to where the old Custer Valley Mall had been. It wasn't a path Nikka had ever used before, but she found herself there now. Now, on what felt like a summer evening where dusk had just passed and the stars were fighting to be seen over the dimming indigo sky.

But it wasn't summer. She wasn't sure when it was—that was hazy in her mind—add to that, she had no idea how she got there; Nikka was pretty sure this was a dream. That meant the creatures were coming. They might not have been in sight at the moment, but they were coming.

"This way," a voice came from ahead. It was feminine and young, and as Nikka glanced upriver, a woman stepped onto the stone path from behind a tall blue spruce.

She had sleek, black hair, and it swayed as the breeze passed. She wore jeans and a white shirt, every bit of her unassuming, yet there was a draw to her that Nikka didn't understand.

She walked toward the woman and scanned the riverbank on both sides. She searched the trees, the water itself, and below the 12th Avenue bridge up ahead. The monsters were going to come from somewhere; it was only a question of from where.

"It's okay," the woman said as Nikka caught up. "You're safe for now."

Nikka couldn't help but cock her head to the side and question. How did the woman know? And what was she up to?

"I understand being skeptical," the woman said. She gestured for Nikka to walk with her along the path, and as they began, everything beyond the trail and the river seemed to change. The giant lot that held the defunct mall became a field of tall grasses and wildflowers. The bridge ahead faded away. The gas station on the corner, the Taco Dave's, the streets and stoplights all either disappeared or reverted to meadows, pines, or boulders. It was like they were walking along the river years before the town of Custer Falls had existed.

The woman watched Nikka's eyes trace their new surroundings. "It's just a young night in a much quieter place."

Nikka couldn't help but smile. She didn't know if it was the change in atmosphere or something in the woman's voice. There was a soothing quality about it all, and though this was all strange, she had already told herself she was dreaming. Dreams were often strange.

"Where are we going?" Nikka wondered aloud. She didn't ask who the woman was. A feeling had grown that she already knew the answer, that this was a close friend. She just couldn't quite remember the woman's name.

"Nowhere in particular. I just wanted to talk." She waved her hand in front as they walked, and it was like the stars came to life. A comet raced through the Milky Way. Constellations pulsed as if waving. The infinite sky beyond was a hue of deep, inky blue Nikka had never seen.

"Okay," Nikka agreed.

They strolled, and though the woman had said she wanted to talk, there was no urgency from either of them. They just enjoyed the night. The smells of fresh lilac, pine, and wildflowers, the warm caress of the summer air on their skins, the embrace of the natural world around them, all calmed Nikka in a way that sleep had not been able to in what felt like an eternity.

The river quieted as they went. They passed into the trees, and Nikka spotted a tiny house up ahead. It was very small, not much bigger than a shed, but in the moonlight it seemed to have a welcoming glow.

"You need dreams like this," the woman said, "dreams that are calm and good for your soul."

"That's the truth," Nikka agreed. "If only."

The woman sat on a log beside the water, water that had narrowed to the size of a small stream. She patted the wood, gesturing for Nikka to join her.

Nikka examined the log, the stream, and the tiny cabin. She was over-whelmed with the feeling of having been there before, of having known this woman before, but she couldn't say how.

She sat. "What's your name?" She was so embarrassed to ask. She should have known the answer.

"My momma called me Masha when I was young, but no one has called me that in a very long time. Most call me Ved'ma."

Nikka thought she remembered hearing the name Masha, but she didn't think it had to do with this woman. It was like it belonged to a long-lost relative or something.

"Which do you like better?"

"Of course Masha. You may call me that."

Nikka nodded and watched the stream bubble as it babbled over rocks and sticks on the bank. The way the water twirled and turned was almost magical, as if the ripples were dancing with the debris and she just couldn't hear the music.

"Masha's a nice name."

"I could help you with your dreams," Masha said.

"I've tried everything. I don't know what you could do that would be any different."

Masha smiled. She leaned forward, waving her hand over the water, and the stream swirled. A small spout rose from the surface, and from inside, a fluttering cloud of lightning bugs emerged.

Nikka couldn't help but giggle.

They straightened into a line, flew up, and did loops. The more they moved, the more they looked like a laser-light show, where their trails made pictures. She saw glowing flowers and explosions of fireworks. She saw a ballet of light and happiness, and she grinned from ear to ear. It made her think of the planetarium she visited with Mom and Dad many years ago, the awe, the beauty, the love they all had together.

Masha waved her hand, and the show dispersed, the swarm of performers vanishing into the trees. "All you have to do is find me," she said, "and we can work out an arrangement."

Nikka watched the last of the glowing yellow dots disappear behind a branch, and she turned to the woman. But Masha was gone. It was only Nikka now, sitting on a log alone in the woods in the middle of the night. Somehow, without Masha there, it seemed so much darker—so much lonelier. Colder, and that cold ran over her skin like lightning.

The shadowy woods beyond the pines felt ominous. The woods were not safe and joyous as they had been. They were threatening. They glared at her from the unseen darkness, plotting and hungering for her.

Nikka glanced around. The small cabin was little more than a pile of rotten logs. The stream was more mud than anything, with only a sliver of water no thicker than what a garden hose would pour. Even the log below her had changed, turning into a worm-riddled hunk of soggy fiber, not something that had once been a tree.

This was no longer a place where she wanted to be.

Nikka stood and heard a crack from somewhere in the forest. It was the sound of a limb breaking, followed by the rustling of debris, and without seeing or hearing another noise, she knew exactly what it was.

They were coming.

She spun the other way and set off along the bank of the stream. There was another crack and a dozen thumps of thunderous footfalls from behind her. They were massive legs pounding into the forest floor. They were heavy and fast. They carried a beast with the purpose of death, and there was no delaying them.

She ran harder, faster, her feet sinking into the moist ground as she moved. She remembered their size and the pain from a thousand other dreams, and she wished Masha was there, that Masha had never left, and that something, anything, could change this dream back to the peaceful stroll it had been just a few moments prior.

Her next step betrayed her. Her right foot sank so far into the ground it was stuck. The bank of the stream had become a bog, and as she pressed with her other foot to free herself, she only sank farther.

"No!"

The mud was cold around her feet. She drifted lower, and the coolness crawled up her legs like tiny frozen fingers. It slurped, and she fought it only to continue lower. She pressed her hands against the ground, and they dove under the surface of the swamp as if she was trying to lift herself by heaving against a swamp of peanut butter.

While she did this, the stomping neared.

She could smell the creature's damp, moldy stench growing closer, and her hands refused to come up from the quagmire.

"Stop it! Stop it! Stop it! Stop it!" she yelled, louder each time.

The footfalls quieted right behind her. She felt the thing looking over her back. She knew the way it moved, and it was hunching over her, rising up and down just barely as it breathed in and out.

She shrieked. It was high and bellowing. It flooded the forest and came back within an echo.

"No—" Fiery pain shot through her neck, and the pointed end of a massive leg burst from below her jaw. She gagged. Her breath was caught in her lungs unable to move. Her throat felt full and wanting at the same time, like she needed to breathe but an enormous meal was clogging the path.

She shook as another leg stabbed her in the back, erupting from her chest. If only she could move. If only she could have called for help (from Masha), maybe this didn't have to happen.

She couldn't help but try to scream again.

The scream came out and her hands jerked free. She spun and grabbed the thing behind her, shoving it away. There was a thud as her head hit the nightstand, and her lamp crashed against the wall and then the floor. She caught a glimpse of what she had pushed as Rich flew backward, his head slamming into the edge of the open door and he sank to the floor.

Pain cradled Nikka's skull. "Rich!" she shouted as she scrambled across her bed and perched at the end.

Rich blinked and nodded. He rubbed the back of his head then stared at Nikka.

"Rich, are you okay?" God, she hoped he was.

There was a streak of red crawling down the corner of the door, and just as she thought, when he brought his hand from the back of his scalp, it was red too.

"Rich, I'm so sorry."

Lynn rushed into the room. She kneeled beside Rich and shot daggers from her eyes at Nikka. "You were screaming. He was checking on you." She saw his hand and the back of his head. "My god, you're bleeding."

"I'm okay." Rich raised a hand. "Just saw some stars."

"You're bleeding!" Lynn screamed. "We're going to the ER to get you checked out. You might have a concussion."

"I'm fine." He tried to stand and fell back on his rear. Nikka felt the impact shake the floor. "Just—give me a minute."

Lynn stared at Nikka. There was so much hate in that look. Nikka felt about an inch tall.

She climbed over the edge of the bed and reached for Rich. "Let me help."

"Stay back." Lynn raised her palm. "Just stay back." She draped Rich's arm over her shoulder and helped him stand. "Let's get your shoes on."

"I don't need a hospital."

"We're going." She led Rich from the room.

That was the last time Nikka saw them alive.

Chapter Four

NIKKA WAS OUT OF the house as the sun started to rise.

The morning air was cold, raising the hairs on the back of her neck. Her hoodie was barely enough to deal with it, but then she was in the car, and she knew the day would warm up, hopefully by the time she reached the forest.

Energy drinks clinked against each other in her bag as she hit the gas. She picked up her coffee mug and sipped. She wiped a tear from her cheek as she turned toward Custer Falls National Forest.

She had sent one text during the night as she nervously paced the house. Rich didn't respond. There was no answer about his condition. He had said he was fine before they left, but why hadn't they come back? Was his head worse than they thought? Yes, there was some blood, but...

Then again, maybe it was just Lynn? She and Nikka hadn't gotten along well since the day Nikka moved in. Rich had told her about the free room one day at work, and it seemed like a win-win for both of them. Rich's rent would go down. Nikka could move out of what was essentially a halfway house where she was stuck after being a minor when her parents died. They worked together so they could carpool if needed to save on gas.

But Lynn was always cold. It was like the woman thought Nikka wanted her man, like Nikka was going to hit on him if they were left alone together for too long.

She had no interest in Rich, not in that way. She hadn't had a single boyfriend or love interest in years, not since the dreams started. Her life just wasn't fit for it. How many guys could be okay with a girl waking up screaming next to them a couple times a night? So she didn't try.

She just hoped so badly that Rich was okay.

Nikka passed the edge of town with her gaze locked on Mount Custer's thinning snowy peak. It was April, and the spring thaw was well underway. She recalled her dream from the night before, the stream by Masha's little cabin being fed by the tail end of the mountain's long-stretching reach. That was what happened, where most of the water in the forest came from, other than a small fork from the Missouri that flowed in all year long.

She couldn't help but think the snow she was looking at would find her at Masha's house once she discovered where it was. That idea stayed with her until she reached the Laurel Trailhead and parked. Then her thoughts shifted to how crazy this trip was.

She was going to hike into a forest looking for a witch from an old legend or a woman from her dreams, whichever she found first, in an attempt to quell her nightmares. It made no sense. It was the type of thing that would get people committed if the authorities found out, yet there she was, ready to dive in.

But what other choice did she have? What other options? She had been living like this for nearly two years and dying a little bit every day because of it. She was going to die for sure if she didn't fix it. She knew that. Especially after what happened to Rich.

Her gut tightened as she thought about him. He was kind to her from day one. He had welcomed her in, knowing she had issues. Granted, he may not have fully grasped what he was getting into, but he took that chance to help her. And then she shoved him across the room into a door.

"I hope he's okay."

With that whisper, she was moving, grabbing her backpack and climbing out. She couldn't sit there and think about it or she was going to start crying. She had to do this no matter how dumb it felt. What was the worst that could happen, anyway? She went on a hike for a few hours and found nothing? She came home with the same dreams and suicidal contemplations she started with?

"Fuck it." She shut the door, hit the locks, and flung the backpack over her shoulder. Maybe it was one step closer to the loony bin for her, but she was going to take it.

Past a bulletin board of notices and through the gate, into the forest she went.

Under an overcast sky, the woods seemed dark. The sun only helped so much, being low and behind the clouds. The shadowy underbelly of the debris-covered floor forced Nikka to think of the dream she was trying so hard to forget, at least the last part of it. She told herself, *There are no bug-people here. This is the real world.* She couldn't help but reply to herself, *You don't go looking for witches in the real world.*

She hiked about a half mile before pulling out her phone. She knew there wouldn't be service out there, but she had taken a half dozen screenshots of maps of the trails and how she was supposed to reach Black Creek. As she scrolled through the images, she verified her plan: left at the next fork, about two miles to a stream, Rocky Bottom, and that was supposed to lead to the start of Black Creek. That was if the thing still existed. Some of the stuff she read online that morning talked about how many of the old streams and runoff paths had shifted over the years with changes in weather patterns and varying snowfalls. But she knew this whole thing was a gamble from the start.

Satisfied she hadn't missed her first turn, she continued down the trail.

The shadows seemed darker the deeper into the woods she went. A breeze whipped past her ears, and it whispered something she couldn't quite make out. It made her think of those girls who got lost out there last spring, and more than ever, she understood how important it was to stay on her path even if urged to go a different way. Because it was like something out in the gloom was calling her to go off trail. She shook her head and forced herself onward. That fork shouldn't have been too much farther.

It wasn't. After a bend in the trail and an incline, there it was. Paths went right or left. A sign directed hikers right for Mount Custer and the lake and left for the Rocky Bottom trail.

"Good." At least so far her navigation skills were paying off.

Left she went, and while walking, she pulled an energy drink from her backpack and gulped it down. Her eyelids were getting heavier, and the last thing she needed was to take a nap out there in the wild.

Caffeine and vitamins rushed through Nikka's veins, and it felt good. It was the pickup she needed to keep her forward momentum. It made her breathe deeper and notice the pine and sage and earth all around her. It made her look up into the trees and spot birds passing overhead. It made her hear the chatter of ground squirrels, likely warning each other of her approach.

She was in a beautiful place, and she resented that she never went out there. But it was rare that she went searching for an ancient witch too.

About an hour down the path, Nikka's trail crossed Rocky Bottom. There was a small bridge over the slim waterway and a little plaque that read the stream's name. This was where she would go off trail.

Nikka took a deep breath and checked her maps again. This was the place. She could see a faint path along the side of the stream; it was light and only a foot or so wide, worn into compressed dirt, unlike the manicured named trails. But she was pretty sure that was the way.

"Here goes." She stepped off the bridge onto the slim line of earth and began walking. She wouldn't have called it the point of no return, but it was. It was the turn that decided the next period of her life. All she knew was that she better watch her ass—from here on out, if she got lost, it was going to be a job for a search and rescue team to find her.

The water's babble and the kaleidoscope of greens and shadows coming through the canopy took Nikka back to something she would rather not have imagined: her parents. The walk by this stream was like so many she had taken with them when she was young, before the hard times when Mom lost her job because the company's owner was murdered by some druggie kid in his office, starting her family on a roller coaster of ups and downs as they tried to rebuild their finances. Back then they would take weekend trips all over the state. They saw Yellowstone, which Dad always had to call Jellystone and laugh. They saw the glaciers up north. They saw the sapphire mines in Philipsburg. They went in the caves in Lewis and Clark County since Bloodtooth was closed off. They were so close, as close as a family could have been.

Her parents wanted her to see everything they could expose her to. How sad they would have been to see her today.

The only time she could ever remember having a problem on one of their trips was on their way to California through Salt Lake City. There was a blizzard as they drove into town.

Huge white flakes piled on the hood and collected under the wipers. Cars flew past them on the highway as Nikka held herself tightly in the backseat—there was never so much traffic in Custer Falls, and definitely not so fast in the snow.

They stopped overnight in a hotel, and Dad rushed her and Mom into the lobby as he went back for the luggage. When he came inside, covered in snow, he brought only the essentials—they were only staying overnight, after all.

Nikka was so glad when they got to the warm, cozy hotel room that she bounced from bed to bed, giggling. Mom and Dad played games with her and snuggled as the night moved on and it was time for rest.

A twig snapped under her feet, and it occurred to Nikka that that trip was the last one they took before her mother lost her job. It was also one of the oldest nightmares she could still recall.

It didn't matter that they were out of the snow and traffic for the night or that Mom and Dad were in the queen bed on the other side of the nightstand. When she closed her eyes that night, she was right back in that freeway traffic, snow building on the roads and the bitter cold beyond the glass creeping ever inward. It froze the windshield wipers still. It turned the roadway to ice. Nikka watched the cars outside slide and crash into one another, saw windows shatter and metal crumple as one driver hit another.

Blood splashed and froze in strange shapes on the glass and then the roadway, and when Nikka screamed and reached for Mom in the front seat, Mom was gone. She turned to Dad, and Dad was gone. She was alone in a car at highway speeds, barreling down the slick ice, and all she could do was cry and grip the seat with all her might.

It wasn't anything like her dreams to come yet she opened her eyes crying. She never even wrecked inside that runaway vehicle.

The next morning, though, that was when their trip took a sour turn, and she would never forget it.

They ate in the hotel; there were sausages and waffles. They checked out and went to the vehicle only to find the rear of the family hatchback had been smashed in. Glass covered the snowy ground and the rear of the car. Bags were open, their contents tossed across the car, and Mom's bag was completely gone.

Thieves had come in the night, smashed up their car, gone through their things, and taken what they wanted. Once the sight sank into Nikka's mind, when it no longer looked like an accident but she understood what had happened, it was worse than the cold feeling in her dream. It wasn't an impending crash that was coming; the crash had already happened. Someone had smashed into their lives and showed her that nothing of hers was sacred, nothing could be protected. It was a lesson in might makes right, that if you were sneaky and mean and strong enough, you could rip whatever you wanted from the arms of others.

She was a babe in a world full of monsters, and anything they wanted was theirs. She would find out years later that included her parents. It included anything she wasn't strong enough to fight for.

Nikka hiked, refusing to let herself cry. She always cried when she thought of Mom and Dad. That was why she tried to think of them as seldom as possible. But in these woods, following this stream, there was something helping to hold those tears back. A warning light flashed inside her brain, disrupting the sadness, because something bigger was happening that she couldn't put her finger on yet.

The stream was narrowing and the ground was softening. It wasn't quite mud like in her dream, but it did compress under her feet. The floor was flush with green. Mosses and grasses covered the ground where it was hard, crumbled stone just feet prior. The trees appeared greener, even under the overcast sky and the shadowy canopy.

It was where the stream split, and without looking at her screenshots of maps, Nikka knew right where she was. The split to her right was Black Creek.

Chapter Five

Nikka's heart fluttered. She was on the right path. She didn't know if there was a woman ahead or if she could help, but she knew this was the way.

The water running down the creek was energetic. It was happy water, if there was such a thing. It was running to its new home to say hello to the path ahead, and the bright greenery around Nikka seemed ecstatic to have it. It was like she was walking into a scene from *Snow White*, where Custer Falls National Forest had become a kind of vibrant, magical place, and it felt good.

Her pace increased. Her heart pumped. At that moment, she wasn't even tired. It was like this path opened up something inside her that was at once invigorating and soothing. She knew whatever lay ahead was waiting just for her. It wanted to help her despite a soft whisper inside her gut that warned that this was too good to be true. It warned with a phrase her economics teacher said on the first day of class: *There's no such thing as a free lunch; someone's always got to pay.*

That warning was rational, she knew that, but she told herself it had to be an overreaction because everything around her told her to continue on with a smile on her lips. Wildflowers bloomed by the creek bed. Sunlight shimmered on the narrow stream, and its reflections danced across the underside of nearby pine boughs like joyous flares of frolicking fairies.

Then she saw the log and ran to it. It was just like the one in her dream—the first time she saw it, not the nightmare version. She held out her hand to touch it because it seemed too strange to believe—strange and wonderful. It was an object from a dream, and that didn't make sense—but somehow, here, it did. The idea made her mind buzz with the possibilities, with hope. It was a feeling she hadn't felt in almost two years, not since the doctors told her they could help her, not since she was starting the drugs and sleep therapies and clinging to the idea that they could fix her. They didn't, but somehow, she knew what was nearby could. She just knew it.

She reached for the log, but she didn't have time to touch it. Her eyes couldn't wait, and even as her fingers stretched, her gaze found the little log shack by the tree line.

It was tiny, but it was beautiful. Small logs made up the walls, and chunks of shake shingles covered the roof. Green mosses sat like a puffy cloud over the top, and vines with dangling pink and red wildflowers trimmed the lines of the roof and festooned like banners from its corners. A thin line of black smoke rose from a stone chimney toward the rear, and this was the last, most beautiful thing. This meant *she* was home!

Nikka ran across the gap to the door. She paused there, drawing a blank on what to do. Knock? Call out?

She smelled something savory coming from inside. It was like a warm, meaty soup, and she instantly wanted some.

She would knock. That was the polite thing to do.

Nikka raised her first and moved it toward the door, and it swung inward, revealing the smiling face from her dream.

It was Masha. She wasn't exactly as her dream suggested, but she looked damn close. Her clothes were not quite modern—no tapering jeans and slim-fit top. She wore a white blouse that was loose and flowing in the breeze that carried that amazing smell from inside. A white skirt hung from her hips, almost to the floor. It covered all of her except her bare, pink toes, which poked out from under the hem.

Masha smiled as she brushed her black hair across the long dangling pendants of her necklace and over her shoulder. She opened her mouth to speak, and that feeling of familiarity from the dream world overwhelmed Nikka.

"Nikka." Masha smiled with her face and her words. She raised her arms wide, reaching and waving Nikka inward.

Yes, was all Nikka could think. *Yes.* It was her long-lost friend, a relative she hadn't known she needed or even existed, and *Yes* repeated. Nikka stepped into her arms, and they embraced. There was love there. It radiated from Masha. It soaked into Nikka like a gushing fountain.

There was a small sting on the back of Nikka's neck, tiny, little more than a mosquito bite, and Masha pulled away, saying, "Come in, come in."

Nikka ignored the pain. She must have caught a hair on something. She stepped inside the tiny cabin and shut the door behind her. It latched with a small piece of metal that slid over a slot in the wood. When she turned back, she saw Masha rubbing her fingers over a pot that sat on top of a small woodstove in the back of the room.

Nikka took in the one-room cabin.

A narrow wooden bed was on the left. A large bag-looking mattress lay there, lumpy and layered with colorful blankets and furs. On the right was a small table with a single chair. On the table was a single plate and a single fork, a few unlit candles, and a pile of very old papers.

It was an old place, she could see that, but it wasn't in any way rundown. Each item in the room was from an older time, outdated by modern standards, but still, they all looked nearly new, from the blankets that could have been at home in a rustic, old west novelty store, to the solid black stove, to the papers with rough edges but not a water or age mark on them.

If Nikka didn't know any better, she would have thought she had traveled there in a time machine.

"Sit," Masha told her. She motioned at the only chair and picked up a metal cup from a small shelf on the wall. "You've had a long walk. You should rest."

Nikka didn't want to be rude, so she sat, though the idea of rest made her shiver. Rest meant relax, and relax was too close to sleep. She forced her spine straight and her head high to keep any thoughts of sleep as far away as possible.

Masha stirred and lifted a ladle from the pot. She poured a thick concoction into the cup and walked to the bed with it held tightly between her interlocked fingers. She sat and looked Nikka up and down.

"Your dreams are tearing you apart," the woman said.

A jolt shot down Nikka's nerves. Yes, her dreams were. Or had already. It was obvious to those who knew her, but as this woman looked at Nikka, it felt like she was seeing right through her.

The whole thing was insane. They only knew each other from her dream, but here they were, face to face, a real meeting in a real place. Unless Nikka was still dreaming and she was about to wake up in the loony bin.

"This is real, I assure you," Masha said. Nikka stiffened, and Masha continued. "No, I'm not reading your mind—it's written on your face. It is magic, though.

"Magic is real. And dreams are magic, in a way. That's why I was able to visit you last night. That's why you knew you needed to find me."

Nikka glanced around the small cabin again. It was warm, and the fire popped inside the stove. She tried to make sense out of this place because she had not traveled back in time. This woman was not the Black Creek Witch—that was a hundred years ago. A legend. This woman had to be some kind of survivalist, an eclectic, off-grid fanatic who wanted to live like they did in the old days. The word—magic—made everything kind of hiccup. The idea of magic being real was where her gears got stuck. Sure, people believed in crystals and tarot and even Wiccan abilities, but they were all kind of *out there* from the way Nikka thought the world worked—and those seemed mild compared to what this woman was saying.

"Magic?" Nikka had to ask. "What do you mean?"

"Oh, it's a lot less complex than it sounds." Masha smiled wide. "I just know some of the old ways that can help, especially with dreams. You see, dreams are how the energy in our body expresses itself. We can use that to shape our world if we wish, and we can use other energies to affect our dreams.

"I'm sure before this mess with your nightmares you'd had dreams of your future. You'd had moments of déjà vu. Those are moments when your dreams are connected to the waking world and either informing your conscious mind or influencing it.

"Over the years, I've learned to harness those moments and direct them. I can do that to help you with your problem."

Harness dreams? It didn't make sense, but at the same time, the woman obviously had the ability to put herself inside Nikka's dreams, so there could have been something there. And the idea that Masha could be right, that she could really stop the nightmares?—that unleashed a flood of hope that Nikka had a hard time holding back, however silly the woman's proposition was.

"So, how?"

Masha lifted the cup in her hands. "This starts the process."

"Like, a potion?"

"You can think of it like that if you wish. It is a blend of natural herbs and mushrooms from this forest that will connect to your dreams and let me help pull back the layers of trauma you're holding onto. It's only a first step, but once you start, you will immediately feel the difference the next time you sleep."

Nikka's heart beat faster. The prospect of a better life, of being free of these burdens, made her want to leap forward and guzzle down the contents of that mug, regardless of not knowing what was inside it. But she knew there was more to it. *There's no such thing as a free lunch.*

"What does it cost?"

Masha smiled. It wasn't as warm as her past smiles; there was something below the surface. But it wasn't quite sinister, either.

"I need some help. There are things I need done outside of the forest which I cannot do. You will do those things for me. After this first dose—" She raised the mug. "It will take four more to completely rid you of your nightmares. One per week. You do the tasks I ask. You come back once a week for the next dose. And in four weeks, you will forever be free."

Nikka had to restrain herself from moving toward the woman. She wanted that drink right now. She was desperate for it, no matter what the cost, no matter what answers Masha may have to any other questions she posed. But she held on for the moment.

"So, I work for you... for a month?"

"Yes."

"And your *potions* stop the nightmares?"

"Yes."

"Forever?"

"Yes."

"Forever forever? Like they won't come back in a month and I'll have to come get more?"

"Gone forever. And then you will never see me again."

That was what she wanted to hear. She didn't want to turn into a junkie for whatever was in that tin cup.

"What are the jobs?"

"Mostly picking things up and delivering things. Simple tasks. Nothing too hard."

"Anything illegal?"

Masha shrugged. "Nothing that will get you in trouble if you follow my instructions."

That was vague. But if it was true, it was something she could deal with.

"Are you interested?" Masha tilted her head. She held the mug in one hand, swirling the contents. "Four weeks to complete relief?"

"Yes." There was no other answer. There was no more thought that needed to happen. Nikka knew she was likely months away from suicide, if not closer, and she needed help, some kind of lifeline to fix this problem.

What's the worst that could happen? she asked herself. The dreams come back? She dies? Both of those were already on the table. She had to do this.

Nikka stood and walked toward Masha. Masha held the mug high for her to take.

Nikka accepted the container and raised it to her mouth. She smelled it as the rim touched her lips but took no time to analyze the scent. There was something like grass, maybe, something a little spicy, like cinnamon, and something metallic.

She tipped it back and let it flow over her tongue to the back of her throat, and her taste buds confirmed every scent. A little spice, a little metal, something like sour vegetables, and a texture that was thick and a bit grainy.

Nikka couldn't have cared less about the taste. It could have tasted like burnt dog shit and she would have drunk it with the hope of more in a week.

She needed this to work. It had to work.

The potion slipped down the back of her throat, and though it was warm from the pot, what she felt was cold. It crept around her throat and up her spine to her brain. It went down her neck to her chest. It encircled her and flushed her body with a chill and then a wave of tingles.

She sighed as it sank, and her eyes closed involuntarily. When she opened them, she saw not a fresh and orderly cabin, but she was standing in the middle of a pile of rotting wood. Moss and mud made the floor. There was no Masha, and the air smelled foul and moldy. Her heart fluttered, and she blinked.

There was Masha. There was the cabin. Everything was back where it was supposed to be, and as the drink reached her belly, Nikka breathed deeply with relief. She didn't know what that vision was, but it was gone, and that was all that mattered. She had hope now. She was on the way to living her life again.

She smiled and handed the cup back to Masha.

"Now, what do I do? What's the first job?"

Masha stood. Her posture urged Nikka toward the door. "You go home. You rest. The dreams will be better—not perfect, that will come with time. When you wake, I will send you the first task."

Nikka opened the door. Masha smiled, and Nikka stepped outside.

"Go rest, my girl," Masha said.

Rest, Nikka thought as she hiked toward her car, hope overflowing inside.

Chapter Six

WHEN NIKKA RETURNED HOME, she didn't see Rich or Lynn. She didn't know if they were still at the hospital, in their room, or out doing something. She thought about sending Rich another text but didn't. He hadn't responded to the last one. She decided to give him time and wait. Besides, for the first time in way too long, she was excited to get some sleep.

She was buzzing and could think of nothing but sleep.

She showered and slipped on a T-shirt and a pair of loose shorts, closed her door tight, and climbed under her covers. The sheets were cool and welcoming.

Nikka turned off the lamp and looked at the ceiling with both dread and anticipation. She was about to close her eyes and let it happen. Willingly. She had no proof that Masha knew what she was talking about, no real reason to believe this was going to work, and part of her was terrified that it *wasn't* going to work. Still though, she had hope, and it was strong. It was a crazy thing, but it was there.

With her heart pounding in her chest, Nikka closed her eyes. She breathed deeply and wiggled, letting the sheets enshroud her, letting her blanket weigh down over her limbs and hug her, pull her into a comforting embrace the way it used to and soothe her into—

Her view was her room, but not in the apartment she shared with Rich and Lynn. She was in her old room, back in the house with Mom and Dad, and she was lying in her old bed, staring at that ceiling. It was popcorn, hanging from the drywall in tiny, matte-white clumps.

She was back in the place where it all started, and she knew what day it was.

Nikka closed her eyes and shook her head. This was a mistake. Why was she asleep again? She clenched her fists and screamed, "Wake up!"

But she didn't. She was still there, and worse than that, when she opened her eyes, she wasn't in bed anymore. She was standing by the window, looking out over the backyard and into her neighbor Sully's yard.

No!

The creature was there. It was easily ten feet tall, and it tossed dirt behind it as its enormous front insectoid legs slammed into the ground and scraped. It dug, and Nikka trembled. She knew that at any moment it was going to yank Sully from some underground bunker, lift him up, and then it would see her.

It reached down as she predicted. It raised up her neighbor. They fought, and another beast held the girl. Sully slipped free and attacked the other one. He and the girl escaped over the fence.

Nikka shivered. What was going to happen was inevitable. It happened every time she relived this dream. There was no escape.

But it didn't. The creature never looked her way.

When the event was over, it just kind of disappeared.

Nikka's jaw hung. She could barely believe what had just happened. She was in her old room, looking out the window at a beautiful day and... And she was okay.

She was okay.

More than that, she was great. She knew her mom and dad were in the house as they had been that day. They hadn't seen what she saw, but they were there.

Nikka turned and rushed from her room. "Mom! Dad!" Her feet carried her through the hall then down the stairs.

She found them both at the kitchen table. Dad had a bowl of cereal and a slice of toast. Mom had an onion bagel with a white spread over its top. They each had steaming cups of coffee.

Nikka grinned like an idiot. Her heart leaped with joy. She held herself still as she weighed the moment and prayed this was real and not some cruel trick, that it wasn't all a setup and the beasts weren't waiting to burst through the back door and kitchen window.

But they didn't.

She ran around behind them and pulled one parent close in each arm. Mom smelled like Mom, her citrus shampoo, the scent of her lotion. Dad wore his weekend scruff, and his prickly face rubbed on hers. It was perfect, as perfect as a dream could be when someone hadn't had a good one in years.

"What's going on?" Dad asked. He frowned as he looked her over.

"Are you okay?" Mom added. She squinted and cocked her head.

Nikka slowly released them and backed away, just enough to give them space. "I—I just love you guys."

It was like time had reversed and she was standing in a place she should have remained, should have enjoyed and held onto back then. She felt herself tearing up.

She spent the day with them. They went to the park, the ice cream shop, and finished at the bowling alley. They hadn't bowled in years, not since she was in a preteen league, and the feeling was that of being whole again. She was where she was supposed to be. They did all those things together as a family, and it warmed her being like nothing had in so very, very long.

That evening, they were sitting in the living room and playing Scrabble. She was on the floor beside the coffee table with a cup of cocoa even though it was warm out. She could drink hot chocolate endlessly then—before her beverage of choice was coffee at any hour. Mom had tea and sat comfortably on the couch, just far enough from Dad that they couldn't see each other's tiles.

A knock came at the front door. Nikka's father stood, and as he walked toward the entryway, an eerie feeling rose inside Nikka. After such an amazing day, it was hard for her to recognize it at first, but it was there, and her only thought was *Stop*.

It was late reaching her lips.

Dad was opening the door, and from the other side, thick, monstrous legs burst through. They smashed the door into the wall and snagged Dad's arm with the tip of a giant limb.

They were back. The monsters were back!

It scurried into the house, thumping on the floor as it hauled Dad along by his pierced, bloody arm. Red trailed behind them, and Dad mopped much of it up with his dragging clothes.

Mom screamed, and a leg punctured her chest. She gagged and hitched as she tried to suck in air. It yanked her across the room, and... Nikka was frozen.

The monster's head wobbled and leaned toward her. Its mandibles clacked and twitched, eager to taste her.

The front window crashed inward, glass and shards of frame raining onto the carpet. Insect legs crawled inside.

She cried. Her hands clenched. This wasn't supposed to happen.

She opened her mouth to scream, and a massive limb shattered her teeth, ripped her mouth wide, and cracked her jaw in three places as it shot down her throat.

Nikka jerked and her eyes shot open. She was in her room in the apartment. Light came through the blinds and lit the space in streaks of morning amber. She was safe and warm inside her bed. She breathed and looked at her phone, and she couldn't believe what she saw.

She had slept for eighteen hours.

The moments with her parents—she remembered them vividly—passed like they had been in real-time. She teared up as she remembered each event, each hug, each moment that, while it had never happened, was time she had wished for since their deaths. It had all ended in blood, but it had been amazing. It was a night's sleep, a real night's sleep, and an experience that she was so, so grateful for.

And she had slept. She stretched, and for the first time in forever, she felt rested. For the first time in a long time, she didn't fear that closing her eyes would send her into a dream of hell without notice. It was a feeling that made her grin, and her brimming eyes poured.

———

Nikka took her time with breakfast.

She made eggs and toast and coffee, and she sat at the table and enjoyed them. She didn't know the last time she had drank coffee slowly and savored its robust smell. She was so used to gulping it down to get the caffeine working it was like a completely different experience.

She ate with a smile and basked in the memory of her dream. It had been amazing. Sure, the last few minutes were terrifying, but that was relatively normal compared to what she had been going through. How could she not celebrate the 95 percent awesomeness that was the majority of her night? She was tempted to go back to bed, not because she was tired but simply for more wonderful dreams.

She couldn't do that, though. She had things to do. She didn't know what they were just yet, but there was an urge in the back of Nikka's mind that told her she had to get things done.

It was something for Masha, whatever it was.

She finished all but a few crumbs of her eggs and all of her toast. She drank the last sip of her coffee, and she rinsed her dishes before setting them in the dishwasher.

Nikka noticed there were no new dishes in the dishwasher—or the sink. That meant Rich and Lynn hadn't eaten at home.

Had they been home at all? She hoped the answer didn't mean they were still mad at her.

She walked down the hall and listened by their closed door. It was quiet. There was no talking or snoring or even a TV.

She would text Rich again later. If he didn't text back, she would call him. She had given him enough space; she needed to touch base and make sure he knew how sorry she was and that she was making changes. He would be happy about that.

But first, she had an errand to run.

The Subaru felt like a different vehicle when she sat in the driver's seat and slid the key into the ignition. It seemed larger, the whole world did, without viewing it through the tunnel vision of exhaustion. The spring sky lit the town in sunlight that made her want to lay in its glow and bask.

It wasn't just a new day; it was like she was in a new world.

But she had no time to sit around and marvel. She had a job to do, a *task,* as Masha put it.

Nikka turned the key and backed out of the parking space. She had only given a brief thought to how Masha would send her the work she wanted done, but now she understood she needn't have worried about that. She felt a pulling sensation telling her which way to drive, so she turned west on 12th Avenue, and though her destination wasn't clear just yet, she knew Masha was sending her where she was supposed to go.

If it had been any other day, Nikka would have questioned it. If she hadn't just had the best night's sleep in forever, she would have been more apprehensive about strange urges in her mind willing her to go places. But magic had done it. She couldn't believe she was accepting that as a fact, but yes, it was *magic*. That was what it took to fix her. And magic was guiding her to her assignment.

Nikka felt the pull again. She turned onto Spruce, north this time, and she could feel the anticipation building in her chest. Her fingers thrummed the wheel. The corners of her mouth were rising. She didn't know what the job was, but she was excited to do it. This job was the start of paying for this change, of making it permanent. She didn't know how many jobs there would be, but that didn't matter. It was four weeks of work; that was it. A drop in the bucket compared to how long she had been living without sleep, with her days being controlled by self-induced narcolepsy, by the unrelenting weight of a smothering fear of dreaming. She was thrilled to do this work, to pay off this gift, to make it hers forever.

The sensation was getting stronger. The pull was stiffening, telling her she was getting close. It was like driving home from work, knowing the way instinctively after following the same path so many times that it didn't take thought anymore, combined with the urgency that dinner was ready and waiting for her, and her friends were there, and her party was about to start—all of those things combined into one, and it was crying for her.

There was a building ahead on the corner of Spruce and 7th Avenue, and Nikka knew it was the one she was looking for. She had driven past it on other days but never given it much thought. She studied the nondescript structure, her heartbeat quickening. It was a tan and dark-brown place with a sign that read Ramon and Sons Funeral Home.

"Huh," she said to herself as she followed the pull around to the back of the building.

There was a loading dock and a rear door. To the side was a shed that matched the color of the funeral home. Beside the shed, blocking its view from the road, was a long, black hearse.

Nikka parked beside the hearse, the wheels in her mind spinning, eager yet curious as to what this was all about. What was she doing here? What kind of *task* did Masha want her to do at a funeral home?

Before Nikka could ponder the question, the rear door opened and a middle-aged man smiled at her from the doorway. He wore black scrubs, a rubber apron, and large, black rubber gloves. A splash guard was on his head with the shield tilted up. Almost all of his attire was dripping red.

Nikka didn't know why, but she felt the urge to smile back. She knew it was odd—the man was covered in blood—but she was supposed to like him. It was something subconscious that told her he was a friend, the one she was there to see.

But did she like him? She would have to figure that out.

She opened the door. "Mr. Ramon?"

He took a step toward the car and pointed at it, still smiling. "You'll want to turn around. It'll be easier to load that way."

She didn't ask what she was thinking: *What are we loading?* She just did as he suggested, turning the car around and parking with the Subaru's rear hatch close to the door. When she got out, he wasn't there.

Nikka didn't recall ever doing anything quite so strange—driving across town by feel, pulling into a place she had never been before just so someone she didn't know could treat her like an old acquaintance. And she still had a smile on her face.

"Whatever." She had to do the job, whatever it was.

The door opened, and she knew even before she saw Mr. Ramon carrying out a two-foot-wide rubber tote that she needed to open the rear hatch. She lifted it and stepped aside as he set it in the car. The rear of the vehicle sank as he let go.

"Two more," he said, and she followed him into the building.

The stench hit her like a wall as she passed through the door. It was rank and smelled like wet decay mixed with cheap cherry air freshener. She followed Ramon, telling herself to ignore it while her stomach did somersaults.

They went into the preparation room, a steel-walled space with blood-stained tile floors and multiple drains. She could feel the acts done in this room: embalming, organ removal or storage, make-up, dressing, and things worse that hung in her mind in clouds of intentional ambiguity. There were things that happened there that she just couldn't dare to imagine right then.

Two rubber totes exactly like the one Ramon had put in her car sat on a stainless-steel table. Those were why she was there, and she didn't want to touch them.

"There they are." He picked up the next one and winced as he did it. "Can you grab that one?" He nodded at the last container.

"Yeah." Nikka paused. It was the first time today she was hesitant. There was definitely something there that her gut—her real gut, not the sensation she had been following—was telling her to back away from. It was telling her that what was going on there wasn't right.

But it was just a tote. It was just a container, and she was just doing a task—a small thing as payment for the most wonderful gift. She just had to do it, regardless of how she felt, and things would be fine.

Nikka wrapped her fingers around the handles and lifted. She groaned. The thing had to weigh forty pounds. She imagined she was at the gym. It was a workout, and she could do it.

The contents shifted as she walked to her car. It was slight, but she could feel thick, loose items jostling around as she carried the container, and a slimy feeling slid up her arms.

At the car, Ramon took the tote from her and set it in the back. They were all in a line, one, two, three, and the sight of it made Nikka's stomach twitch inward. There was something off about whatever was in those, and she didn't want to ask—she was afraid to ask, afraid the answer could drive her away from her goal.

Ramon closed the hatch. He gave her a grin. "That does it. Thanks for the help."

"Yeah. You're welcome."

She turned toward the front of the car, and Ramon said, "Oh, one more thing."

Not one more thing. Her stomach was growing more upset. She wanted to finish whatever this task was and be done with it.

"Here." He pulled the glove from his right hand, revealing a bloody bandage where his pinky should have been. He reached into his pocket and drew out a black plastic bag. Something was in that bag, the weight of it making it swing as he held it out for Nikka to take.

That slimy feeling only spread. It was up to her shoulders now.

She grasped the bag with two fingers. She didn't want to, but it was part of the task. She had to.

"Okay." Ramon turned and went inside. She thought he may have been humming.

Nikka heard the door shut and lock as she stared at the hidden, dangling contents of the plastic bag. She knew what was in that bag, and she wanted to puke, her stomach making itself known loudly this time.

She took the baggie with her into the car and dropped it on the passenger seat. Unfortunately, the task wasn't over yet.

Chapter Seven

NIKKA COULDN'T STOP THE shivers from running down her spine every time she looked in the rearview mirror or over her passenger seat. She couldn't help thinking, *What have I gotten myself into?*

Neither of those things was strong enough to make her change course.

She had to get the job done. She felt better today than she had in years; she was actually thinking about the future—where she might want to travel, getting a boyfriend, going to a real, in-person university. The idea of killing herself to end the madness was gone—gone from her mind.

The new question was: how far would she go to never return to that awful place?

She hadn't reached that limit yet, not with a few ambiguous totes and a mysterious bag. They gave her the creeps. They made her hope she didn't get pulled over and have to explain what she thought was in those containers. But she was still willing to do this, however weird it was, if it meant saving her life and her future.

She was following the same guide that had taken her to the mortuary. She assumed it was Masha, somehow, but she wasn't sure exactly how it worked. Was Masha watching her drive by means of some sort of crystal ball? Or had she just cast a spell and it was doing the directing? Either way, she didn't want to piss off the witch or the spell, so she was trying hard to listen.

She was practically on the other side of town, at the corner of Road 12 and Lake, when she turned into a parking lot.

She had never been there either, but she recognized the name on the sign. It was a little warehouse-looking place, one that didn't stand out with its gray exterior. But the sign said Ronald's Meats, and that was a name that everyone in town knew. It was a butcher shop, the place hunters dropped off their deer if they didn't want the hassle of butchering and processing it themselves. With Ronald's, they could just stop by a week later and pick up a box of steaks, sausages, and burger that presumably all came from the animal they had deposited.

She didn't have a deer or elk to drop off, but she was pretty sure Ronald wanted what was in those containers.

Nikka followed the signs on the side of the building that read Hunters with an arrow, and pulled around to the rear, backing her hatch up to a rolling garage door. She had just put the vehicle in park when the door went up, and a big, burly man with a bushy, black beard and a red-stained apron walked out.

He waited for her. It was Ronald, she was sure of that.

She walked over and opened the hatch.

"Hi." It was all she wanted to say. She didn't want to dig herself any deeper into whatever this was.

Ronald looked over the totes and grabbed the one on the right.

Nikka noticed his left hand was bandaged, and it took a lot for her to keep her cool. She wanted to say, *What the fuck?* Maybe back up and get the hell out of there? She didn't want what was coming, but she needed this deal to work.

She picked up one of the totes and followed the giant.

They walked through the garage into a large freezer, where Ronald set the tote on a table. Sides of beef and half hogs swung on hooks. Nikka set her tote beside his and shivered at the blast of cold coming from the air vent.

When she got back outside, Ronald was lifting the last tote from her car. He walked past her into the garage without a single word, and for a moment, she was relieved. Then she saw what was on the floor of her car.

Just inside where the hatch closed, this time in a clear, plastic sandwich bag, was a finger—Ronald's finger. It was large and thick, like the rest of the man. It bled into the bag, but not much. The cut was clean, so clean the thing didn't look nearly as real as Nikka knew it to be.

She spun. She didn't have a thing to say to him, but she knew she had to watch the giant for as long as this event would let her. All she saw were his feet as the garage door slammed down.

Back to the finger. "Shit." She was going to have to pick it up. She couldn't just leave it there in the back of her car. She would have to put it with the other one.

Nikka pinched the bag by the corner with two fingers and carried it to the passenger-side door. Goosebumps covered her flesh, and pinpricks tickled her all over. She opened the door and saw the black bag. She was going to have to open it.

"Shit."

She wanted to toss the things away. She didn't want to do this. But she had no choice. The witch wanted her to do something with them; she just didn't know what yet.

She closed her eyes, sighed, and opened them again. She pried back the opening of the black bag and spotted a sandwich bag with a severed pinky and a small pool of blood inside it.

Nikka clamped her teeth shut and shoved the butcher's bag inside with the other one, then she quickly closed the black one. Resting on her passenger seat, the little baggy looked like she had gone shopping for the perfect little item from some boutique and brought it back in a tiny black sack.

Her stomach lurched, and she caught the vomit just before it left her lips. She swallowed it back down with a burning in her throat.

Back in the driver's seat, she headed toward home.

She was done for the day as far as she could tell. She just had to hang on to those digits until told otherwise.

———————

When Nikka arrived at home with her new fingers, it was just as quiet as when she left. No sound from Rich and Lynn's room, not even the TV.

Now, she was starting to worry. Had his hit on the head been worse than she thought? He had said he was okay, but what if there was some sort of brain injury? She wanted to call, but she needed to deal with these fingers first.

She unboxed a small cooler she had picked up on the way home and filled it with ice, then the fingers, then more ice. She took the cooler into her room and set it on the floor on the far side of the bed, where no one would see it from the doorway. Last, she took a breath and closed her door on the way to the kitchen. As much as her day made her queasy, she had built up an appetite.

With the refrigerator door open, Nikka scanned from shelf to shelf. As her eyes moved from one item to the next, she became aware of a craving for a cheeseburger, and not just any cheeseburger—a Lucky Shot Burger.

Nikka hadn't had a Lucky Shot Burger since Mom and Dad were alive. It was never really her favorite place, but Dad loved his cheeseburgers, so at least once a week, they seemed to have it for dinner. He would grin as he ate, as if he had discovered some lost, forbidden treasure and he was embracing his success. The longer that memory hovered in her mind, the more she knew nothing else was going to satisfy her.

She dropped onto the couch, feet up, and tapped on her phone. There it was, available in her food delivery app. She ordered a Four-Leaf Bacon Burger and medium fries with an estimated delivery time of thirty minutes. She didn't really want to wait that long, but she didn't want to go back out, either, so she placed the order.

She tried calling Rich. No answer. She hoped he wasn't blowing her off, so she left a message. He was special to her. He had believed in her, taken a chance on her when he didn't have to. She really hoped they could repair whatever was going on between them.

With her head on a bunched-up blanket, she turned on the television and started an episode of *Lost*. She stared at the jungle greenery and pitied those poor people, and her eyes drifted shut.

Mom sat on the beach, the plane wreckage all over the dunes and fire in the tropical trees beyond. Dad walked from the water carrying a large paper bag that read Lucky Shot Burger in hand; the other hand was missing all five fingers. He didn't seem to mind.

Nikka and Dad sat on the beach beside Mom, and he handed out food to each of them. Mom got a fish sandwich, and Nikka got the bacon burger, the Four-Leaf Bacon Burger, just like Dad. They all smiled.

Nikka could feel the heat from the fire. She could smell the salty ocean air. The crackle of flames and the crash of the waves were all there, but none of that meant anything. What did, what was important, was the fact that she was with her parents and they were happy.

Dad's burger was soaked with blood from his stumped fingers. He ate with his usually ferocious appetite and his thrilled expression at getting his weekly treat.

Mom took a bite and reached for Nikka. She brushed Nikka's loose locks behind her ears and caressed her face.

"You're so much prettier when you show your face." Mom spoke in Russian, which Nikka hadn't tried to use since she was in grade school, but the words rang in her mind as clearly as English.

"*Mom*." Nikka felt herself blushing.

"She's right," Dad agreed between bites.

There was an explosion down the beach. It made the sand shake. People screamed. None of them turned or paid it any mind.

Nikka bit into her cheeseburger. There was a bloody taste to the meat, but she didn't care. She had everything she wanted right now.

From up the beach, a blonde girl was walking toward them. Her pants were ripped, and only one sleeve was attached to her shirt. Blood streamed from one ear, and her face was red from burns. Even with all her injuries, Nikka thought she recognized her. When the girl reached Nikka and her family, carrying a second Lucky Shot Burger bag, Nikka could clearly read the name tag on her chest: Lillian.

Yes, she knew Lillian Martin from ninth and tenth grade. They had been somewhat friends on the school's volleyball team but lost contact after... everything.

Lilly set the bag down in the sand in the middle of Nikka and her parents. "You forgot part of your order." She smiled and continued down the beach.

Nikka was sure they had everything. They could only eat so much.

"Thank you!" Mom called after Lilly. She set her sandwich in the sand and picked up the new bag. She had to unroll the top to get it open, and when she looked inside, she grinned.

"Oh, that was so nice of her!" She pointed the open end at Dad, and he grinned as well.

They both reached into the bag, their hands coming out with chunks of raw meat in their grips. They held the red cuts up and eyed them before shoving them into their mouths.

Nikka giggled. She took a bite of her burger as blood flowed from the corners of Mom's and Dad's lips, and wet, gushing sounds leaked from each chomp. She took another bite and glanced at her food.

She knew she should have been disgusted by what she saw, but instead, she took another bite. The fingers crunched in her mouth as her teeth ripped through bone. Blood ran down her throat as cheese and bacon smushed around her tongue with salty deliciousness.

They all grinned together, and something sounding like a door knock came from the forest.

"You better get that," Dad told her.

She didn't want to. She was so happy right where she was. Why would she get up and answer a door when she had this?

"Go on," Mom said. "We aren't going anywhere."

Another round of knocking.

Nikka swallowed her bite and opened her eyes. Her Lucky Shot Burger was there.

Chapter Eight

LILLIAN'S EYES OPENED TO the inside of her toilet bowl, and she puked. She hadn't realized she had passed out, but she had been vomiting so hard it made sense.

Her stomach ached. Her throat was sore and burning. Her chest prayed to breathe again as bile poured over her lips and splashed into the water. She thought her stomach was empty an hour ago, but here she was again, cramping and vomiting.

Her muscles relaxed. She pulled herself away from the bowl and leaned back on her hands. Her face was so flushed she was sure she was bright red. But maybe she was done for now?

Lilly pulled the handle and wiped her lips before closing the lid and sitting. It was more comfortable than the floor. She hadn't cleaned the bathroom in a month, so the whole thing was likely covered in specks of vomit from what seemed like a thousand times she had bent over that bowl since she made the pact.

She wondered if what she felt in that dream was real. She thought she knew the girl; Nikka, she thought her name was. If that was who she needed to kill next, she was ready for it.

Lilly took a deep breath and stood from the toilet. She wandered back into her living room and glanced from the man to the woman. He was tied to the recliner, the one she used to enjoy but was excited to get rid of now. With so much blood, she was going to have to burn the whole apartment down when the deal was over.

The girl was on the dining room table, the one she and Adrian had rescued from the dump when they conned their way into this apartment. That would burn too. There was no way she could restore it after the blood and cleaver gashes and tiny bits of flesh she was sure had been pounded into the grain.

The man made muffled sounds. Lilly knew what they were, some incarnation of, "Please, let us go?" She had heard it too many times since her pact not to recognize it. But letting them go just wasn't possible.

"It'll be over soon," she told him as she picked up the cleaver beside the woman's severed foot. "Try not to worry."

Lilly raised the cleaver and brought it down below the woman's knee. Raised it again and lopped off the foot on the other leg, then the other knee.

The man in the chair, Rich, she thought his name was, screamed into his gag. Blood ran across the table and dripped onto the floor. Not that much was left after she took the first foot and let the woman drain, but it came.

She dropped the lower legs into a tote on the floor and got back to it. Upper legs, forearms, upper arms, all chopped and into the tote.

Rich was crying. His eyes were closed, and snot was stopping up his nose.

Lilly wanted to feel bad for him. She wanted to let him go and run away. She couldn't do that. She wasn't done yet, and the witch would know it. The witch would find her. She had to finish the job.

She hated how dead inside this deal had made her.

She took a large industrial trash bag from the side table and put it over the woman's head. It was a shame—she was pretty. She pulled the bag down over the woman's bare chest and hips, tightening the opening once the head and torso were inside.

Lilly couldn't help groaning as she lifted the awkward bag and took it into the bedroom, where it would live with the others. The woman was definitely lighter without arms and legs, but she was still heavy.

There was a wet, sloppy sound when she dropped the bag on the others. It stirred a ball of flies, which spread around the room and found new perches.

It was almost over. She was happy for that.

She swatted at a fly too close to her face and snarled at the smell.

Almost over.

Soon, she would be moving on to live her life, free from her deadbeat, abusive boyfriend, free from her addiction to crystal, and not a thing in her way. She just had to get through the next few weeks.

Lilly scanned the room of death. Each bag, each pile, reminded her of someone, all the way back to the far wall, where Adrian sat, the only one she hadn't dismembered and bagged. She enjoyed looking into his dead eyes each time she passed what had once been their bedroom, the room that held more times getting high and more rapes than she dared to count.

She turned back to the living room.

She was taking too long, and the ceiling was running black with oily slime. It wasn't like she could have helped it. She had to eat, and when she ate, she had to puke. It wasn't her plan; it was the witch's. She would only keep down a portion of what she ate, and as the rest came back up, it would bring her addiction with it. It would bring up and expel her weakness, her cravings, and her idiotic lust for the wrong types of guys. But she was almost done.

The oil ran down the walls and puddled. It patted onto the carpet. It slapped Rich on the forehead as he whimpered in his chair. If Lilly didn't act quickly, this was all going to turn south, no matter how close to the end she was.

Black ran into Rich's eyes, and his head twitched. The room's light turned gray. A growl rumbled inside his chest, and his hands clutched the chair.

She had to hurry.

Lilly darted past the man in the chair and stopped at the table. She looked around—where was it? She had just used the cleaver.

"Goddammit."

Rich's skin lost all of its color, turning as gray as the room. His eyes shot open; they were completely black.

"Yes!" She spotted it. The cleaver was hiding on the floor beside one of the totes. She must have set it down while loading them.

There was a ripping sound as Rich tore through his bindings. His hands went out and up. His lips pulled back into a sneer as his teeth ground against one another and black oil ran between them, over his lips, and dripped from his chin.

Lilly ran at Rich, raising the cleaver over her head. He grabbed her shoulder. She brought the blade down as his jaws dove toward her.

She missed the center of his forehead. The edge of the blade sliced through his ear and planted into his shoulder as his teeth sank into her upper arm.

He growled and she screamed. The pain was like nothing she had ever felt. The ripping of her skin, the burning of the oil inside her open wound—the pain was worse than Hell.

He jerked his head left and right. She felt his teeth digging deeper into her.

She howled as she yanked the cleaver free.

Lilly didn't have the strength or leverage anymore. Her other arm was worthless below his bite.

He pulled her toward the ground, and she swung the only way she thought she could: toward his neck, toward herself.

She saw the black ceiling looking down on her. She saw the eyes of a thousand magpies as their heads hung through the slime. They were ready to caw and swarm and rip into her dead flesh if she fucked this up.

She saw black faces in the walls. Rodents and mangy, furry, tree-climbing things were poised to run through the oil and converge on her death. She had to make this count.

The blade sank into Rich's neck. He wriggled and drove Lilly down as she pushed it deeper.

Dark blood ran like a river from the hole in his throat, but he slammed her onto the carpet. Rotting hunks of splattered meat were woven into the strands by her head. Dried blood made the fibers cling and scratch.

Lilly knew the blade was where she needed it. It just had to go deeper. She pushed and rocked it back and forth, sawing into him as she howled, as he pulled away, tearing her flesh from her shoulder.

She heaved and had to have cut his arteries because instantly, blood sprayed like a fountain. It covered her hand and blade. It came down, soaking her face. It sprayed up onto the wall, mixing with the oil and streaking the surface in burgundy.

His mouth went slack, and Rich flopped down dead on her chest.

She let her head rest on the carpet and released the cleaver. She only had to blink once before the room returned to its previous state. No cursed animals watching her. No oils running from the ceiling. Just a dead guy on her chest—her responsibility to cut and pack.

Her goddamn arm killed. It was sealed shut with a nasty scar, but it ached and burned.

She let a minute pass before she fought to roll his body off; it must have weighed twice as much as hers. Then she went back to work. She was so close to being done.

Through clouded eyes, Adrian watched the black sludge cover the ceiling and slide down the walls. He listened to the calls of the magpies and the yipping of foxes as the guy ripped his way from his chair and went after Lilly.

Adrian wished he could giggle. He did it in his mind since his flesh was unresponsive.

He wanted Lilly to get hers. He wanted to see that guy rip her to pieces and take her down. She had had no right to gut him the way she did. All he wanted was a little piece of ass, and she went off the deep end, shoving that kitchen knife in his stomach thirty-seven times. And then she just sat there and watched him bleed out. She didn't try to call paramedics or nothing.

He deserved better than that.

He was her man. He deserved to be respected. He deserved his piece of ass whenever he wanted it, whether she was into it or not. Whether he was high or she was high or whatever. That was her job. If his dick was hard, she needed to take it.

And here she was, fighting another dude.

Adrian watched her blood spray and run down her arm. This guy just had to keep it up and they would be home free, all of them. That witch had said so—if Lilly died, if Lilly fucked up, he got to live.

He had been sitting in their bedroom after rotting for several days. He was the only one in there then, and Lilly shoved a guy through the front door. Adrian struggled to see what was happening until she stabbed the man and he fell into the bedroom doorway. She dragged him away, and between the time when she started chopping and the time she dropped his bagged-up torso in with Adrian, he listened to the witch.

He couldn't concentrate on all of it. It was like the dumb old bitch was reading a goddamn college dissertation. He did listen to the part where she said he could walk again one day. He could come to the woods and serve her.

While Adrian wasn't big on the idea of serving a woman, at that point, he was so tired of being dead and unable to move, of rotting and smelling himself decompose and being able to do nothing about it, of the pain as his brain decayed and his heart dried out, that he would do it. He would work for the witch if she could let him control his own body again. At least, he would work for her until he figured out how to kill her.

And one of the ways she said he could come was if Lilly fucked up her job. And here she was, doing that.

She sliced off the guy's fucking ear, and he was still coming. She hacked into the side of his neck, and he was still coming.

Adrian was starting to like this guy.

In the ceiling, through the blackness, he knew the witch was watching. She was the one bringing in the dark fog and the tall, glowing demons. It was the witch that was making the floor roll and toss oil like a shallow sea as skulls lifted their heads and the giant spiders watched on.

It was like the witch was waiting to see who won. Was she testing Lilly? Or maybe her time was almost up and the witch would have rather killed Lilly than let her walk when her deal was complete?

Either way, that bitch got into the guy's throat.

Fuck.

Blood sprayed and the demons faded. The skulls vanished, as did the fog and the howls.

Lilly got to live—but only for now.

Chapter Nine

NIKKA COULD HAVE CALLED the week that followed her errands a vacation. There were no urges to run any further errands, and her dreams were, well, dreamy. There was always an uncomfortable ending where her nemeses returned, but the nights as a whole were heavenly. She was still worried about Rich and Lynn, but the more time went by, the more their presence was like a memory.

Nikka wasn't motivated to look for a new job. There wasn't a care in her mind other than knowing that tomorrow she was supposed to go back to Black Creek. And that was exciting. That would be her second dose, bringing her closer to peaceful nights being her normal life. She was even thinking of going camping so she could be there at sunup and start the day that much closer to her next dose.

She lay in bed thinking about it, and the more she pondered, the more she knew it was the right choice. She would pack her things, and she would go shopping for a few more—she didn't actually own any camping gear—and she would head out there that afternoon.

A smile broadened on her face, and a hunger gnawed at her belly. She wanted a Lucky Shot Burger.

Nikka could feel the textures of meats and cheeses sliding over her tongue. She could taste the iron flavor of patty juices. She imagined it sliding down her throat, the salty sensation on her lips, and she could no longer hold herself back.

She flipped off the covers and rolled off the bed toward the kitchen. She yanked open the refrigerator door and located her leftover burger from last night right beside the cardboard carton she was now keeping the fingers in—after filling her little cooler twice with ice and her roommates not coming back, she figured she might as well just put them in there.

There was no time to microwave the burger or try to heat it up. She needed that taste in her mouth, so she unwrapped it and plunged it between her lips in a fraction of a second.

The bite was cold, but it was just what she needed. She didn't know why and didn't stop to question it, but for some reason, she had been finding Lucky Shot Burgers irresistible the entire week. They were almost like a drug, so much so that she hadn't gone twenty-four hours without one since the day of her errands.

But Nikka didn't think about that. She had no worries, not after actually being able to sleep this week. She was stress-free. She was, for the first time in two years, optimistic about her future. Why should she spend her time worrying about a few burgers?

She did wonder why she liked them so much, what their special ingredient was, if only so she could make them at home and not have to go out every day. She didn't wonder enough to find out, though.

By noon, Nikka was in her car and on the way to Big John's, the sporting goods store on 10th Avenue. She had only been there once, and that was when she was eight. Her friend Ashley had been selling Girl Scout cookies at the door, and after she bought a box, she wanted to see what was inside.

This time, she went in with fresh eyes. She did a lap just to get the layout, scanning over the outdoor boots, the clothes, the fishing and hunting gear, and finally, the tents and sleeping bags.

She had no idea what she was looking for. Was it a zero-degree bag? A negative-twenty? Was it a square bag or a mummy one? And how did you actually put up a tent? She had seen movies where guys fumbled with poles, and the whole thing really seemed like a mess.

Thankfully, after what felt like a half hour of staring hopelessly at the wall of choices, a saleswoman stopped by and asked if Nikka needed help.

"Jesus, yes!" Nikka blurted out.

The woman smiled and covered her face. She was middle-aged with loose, brown curls highlighted with streaks of gray. She seemed nice enough, and for some reason, Nikka got the impression this lady was also a fan of Lucky Shot Burgers.

"What are you planning?" the saleswoman asked. "Let's start there."

Nikka didn't really want to admit that she was going to see a witch—that would have felt a little awkward, no matter how excited she was for her second dose. What she told the woman was that she was going on a hike that night in the forest, and together they checked the weather and discussed the bags.

It was supposed to get down to the forties that night, and for an extra few degrees of warmth, the woman suggested the zero-degree bags. "I don't know about you, but I'd always rather be warmer," she explained. "You can always unzip it if you get hot."

As Nikka smiled and stared into the woman's eyes, there was a blackness that seemed to leak from below her upper eyelid. It was thick and viscous, almost like oil. But even as she blinked and it ran down her cheek, Nikka held still. She didn't respond to the woman; she only watched the black ooze dripping from her cheeks and running onto her beige vest.

"Everything okay?" the saleswoman asked. "Do you have a color in mind?" Her skin was pale, turning gray. Her teeth were stained with the same oily liquid, but she didn't seem to notice, and her face was shrinking inward as Nikka watched—shriveling up like a dead woman mummifying inside her grave.

Worse than what Nikka saw, though, was what she smelled. There was a wave of stench emanating from the woman. It was the smell of wet rot, like old meat hanging from the bone.

The entire scene made Nikka's stomach lurch. She felt the blood drain from her face as she tried to understand what this person standing in front of her. She wasn't sleep-deprived anymore—it couldn't have been a nightmare, could it? But if it wasn't a dream, what could it have been?

Nikka realized her fingers were trembling. A wind was coming through the store, racing over her neck, and she was cold, so cold, all of a sudden. She had to get out of there.

She spun from the woman, preparing to run, but as she faced the other way, what she saw made her freeze.

A dozen other people stood in the section with them. They were all gray, with black oils running from their eyes. Their faces were dried and sunken—dead. Unlike the saleswomen, though, none of these people had arms.

They were in between the racks of merchandise and in front of every shelf. They blocked every direction Nikka could hope to go. She was debating climbing over a shelf to run when they opened their mouths and screamed.

All at once. It was a wall of pain through gravelly voices, sounds of what must have hurt to speak because the airy vibrations rattled and screeched.

They pained her ears. They made her think of blood and rot and stripping flesh from bone. They made her think of gnashing teeth, and all she could reason from these things was that they were going to eat her if she let them.

Nikka grabbed the shelf and started to climb, and hands pulled on her clothes. It was the saleswoman, the only one with arms, and she was howling something.

Nikka shoved her off and grasped at a higher shelf. She pulled herself up, and the rack came apart in her hands. She tumbled backward with the shelf grasped in her fingers. She screamed as she collided with the floor and screamed again as sleeping bags landed on her and rolled away and screamed again as she scrambled backward and saw she was alone with the saleswoman.

The throngs of corpses were gone. Her head ached, and the saleswoman was at her side, normal, trying her hardest to console Nikka.

It had to have been a dream. Maybe the last dose was wearing off? That had to have been it. She needed to get to Black Creek.

Nikka apologized to the woman and bought the sleeping bag she recommended. She bought a backpack and a single-person tent, and even though she wanted to run from the store in embarrassment, she let the woman teach her how to assemble it and attach everything to the backpack.

With all of it loaded in her car, Nikka stopped at home for some clothes, the gas station for a few snacks, and Lucky Shot Burger for some to-go dinner.

When she reached the trailhead, Nikka was actually pretty confident with everything she had accomplished. She had it all ready, and she was going to do it. But she was still a little shaken by what happened in Big John's. She had thought all that waking nightmare stuff was over. What if it would never be over? What if the problem wasn't just that she needed the next dose? What if it was a permanent thing?

Masha could help. She would have the answer; Nikka was sure of it.

She went to the trunk and got her stuff. She didn't give another thought to her troubles. She was going to be positive and make this happen, and in three more weeks, she was going to be free forever.

———————————

Nikka thought she had plenty of sunlight when she started down the trail, but it didn't take long for the looming dusk to set in, making the entire wooded landscape feel gloomy.

While she could only see the sky through slits and small gaps in the canopy, she could tell it was changing from blue to indigo with reddish clouds. The overhead branches, while initially pleasant and green, were growing blacker and ominous.

A fear rose inside her.

She hadn't seen anything specific that frightened her. It was more of a feeling she was getting. It was like there was something in the woods that was closing in, and even though she had been safe last time, the same might not be true this time.

There was a need for cover. There was a sensation that she needed shelter before it became too dark, and she started searching for a place to camp along the trail, and the sooner she found one, the better.

Nikka flicked on a flashlight to better see the trail. To her surprise, it did little. As night set in, it helped her not trip over the roots and stones that crisscrossed the path, but the light did a poor job of illuminating anything over a dozen feet away. That lack of sight dimmed her excitement even further. It made her wish she had just waited until morning to come out here instead of being so impatient.

"Everything's fine," she told herself.

Something ran through debris in the brush to the right. She pictured claws piercing the dirt and shifting pine needles and broken twigs.

She moved faster.

"There has to be a clearing." She distinctly remembered clearings on this trail the last time she went through there. She just couldn't remember where they were.

"Has to be a clearing," she repeated.

Another scampering sound on the other side, and she moved even faster.

This was no time to get freaked out and excited. She had to keep her head. It was probably just a ground squirrel or something.

She had to keep her head.

Despite her best efforts, she started jogging unintentionally. There was so little light. She couldn't see what the trail was doing ahead. She couldn't guess where the damn clearings were. She had to find one, though. She needed her tent set up, and she needed to be inside it. She just had to keep going.

Keep going.

There was a howl behind her, and Nikka couldn't help but change from a jog to a full-blown sprint.

There were wolves out there. There were bears. There were bobcats and mountain lions. All of those things lived out there, and she was in their home like she was just strolling down the streets of Custer Falls. Was she stupid? What was she thinking going out there alone with no other plan than spending the night closer to the witch?

She would have laughed at her silliness if she wasn't in the middle of it. She was about to laugh out of nothing more than sheer desperation when her light fell on a break in the trees.

It wasn't huge. There was an area about ten feet by ten feet, and the ground was definitely rocky and covered in roots—that wasn't what the lady in Big John's told her to look for—but she had no choice. This was it. This was her camping spot.

Nikka dropped to her knees and pulled her backpack off. She tore the tent from the Velcro straps holding it in place, and, as fast as her fingers could move, she unbagged it and spread it out. She fumbled unfolding the poles. They jingled as she aligned one piece of metal with the end of the next, building the spine that would suspend the tent—

And in the wilderness, there was another howl. Another set of claws shuffling by.

She couldn't tell where they were. Were they a hundred feet away? Or were they ten? She couldn't tell. She only knew she needed this shelter the way she needed air.

One pole through hoops and she seated each end on tiny metal points on opposite sides of the nylon structure. She unfolded the other set of poles and built them into one ten-foot-long pole, sliding it into its loops.

The tiny tent was shaping up to what it had looked like in the store. It stood three feet tall, and as she fastened the ends of the second pole into place, she heard clear growls from the darkness. *Close* growls.

Nikka didn't dare turn around or move more than was absolutely necessary. She didn't waste a breath or an action. She ignored the idea of staking down the tent like she was supposed to and simply unzipped the door, grabbed her bag, and darted inside.

She zipped it shut and fell back onto her ass.

The growls came closer. Something sniffed at the door from the other side, and Nikka sealed her lips with her hands, cupping her face so tightly she wouldn't have been able to breathe if she wanted to. She hoped silence might send them away and knew noises might invite them in.

Her heart pounded. She fought not to breathe but had to. She had to. *Goddammit.*

She let no more than a silent stream pass through her nose.

In and out.

Quiet! Be quiet! she thought to herself. It was her only defense.

The ground outside shifted, crinkled, and snapped, and Nikka clamped her jaws shut.

She would not make a noise. She would not make a noise.

There was another rustle in the trees, this one at least a dozen feet away, and growls turned to barks as whatever was outside her tent took off after it.

Shit.

Nikka sat in darkened silence for a long time. She didn't know how long it was before she had the courage to unroll her sleeping bag and quietly climb inside. It was longer still before she had the stomach to take out one of her burgers and eat it.

The burger, though, it told her it was going to be okay. The familiar feel, the soothing taste. She knew she was finally safe for the night, at least while she was awake.

Chapter Ten

Nikka dreamed she was in the back of a covered wagon as it traveled through the forest. Her mom and dad were in the front, and snow blanketed their path.

She huddled under a scratchy blanket, the cold biting at her fingers and toes as well as her cheeks and ears. Somehow, she was in the days of western settlers, and they were going up a mountain in what had to be winter.

"There!" Mom pointed at a flickering light. She was shivering; they all were. It was hard to see the illumination through the field of white, but it was a flame out in the darkness. It was their salvation from freezing to death if they could get inside.

"Thank God." Dad jostled the reins, and the horses veered to the right toward the light. A minute later, they could see a candle in a window, the window a part of a small cabin. "Let's hope they let us in."

He pulled the wagon to a stop and said, "Let me go check."

"Hurry," Mom told him. She pulled her blanket tighter around herself and watched him climb down from his seat.

Dad was halfway to the cabin when a door opened, letting dancing firelight escape around the silhouetted shape of a very large man. From where Nikka watched, he almost filled the frame, more like a bear than a human. Besides his size, there was something in the darkness that bothered her. Like the light escaped the cabin, a feeling burst from its insides. It was a warning to keep away. It was a sense of danger and evil, and Nikka felt it invading her through the screen of falling snow, through the blanket, through her skin. She felt it in her core that, like the giant bug-men, this man—this whole place—was evil. And Dad was walking right toward them.

"Dad!" Her voice sounded muffled through the shower, even to herself. "Dad, come back!"

He didn't turn. He raised a hand in greeting toward the giant man, and the giant stepped outside.

"Mom, stop him!"

Mom didn't move. She stared at the oncoming interaction and rubbed her hands together. Was she ignoring Nikka?

"Mom! We have to go!"

Mom didn't go. Did she even hear Nikka?

Dad was saying something to the giant, and the giant reached forward, seizing Dad by the neck.

Nikka was way too far, but she heard it. She heard a muffled crack and a gag from her father's throat.

The massive man lifted Dad into the air like he was more toy than human, and Dad swung his feet wildly, grabbing for the giant's face and missing. His arms were too short.

"Dad!" Nikka screamed, but it was like no one was listening.

Unable to reach the man's face, Dad gripped the tree trunk of an arm holding him up. It was like concrete. He slammed his balled-up fists against it.

Nothing.

Fear clamped down hard on Nikka. It pulled her tightly into herself. That may not have been a man-sized insect, but she knew how this was going to end. She was going to lose her dad, and the giant was going to come after her and Mom next.

Dad squirmed, his arms and legs flailing. His jaw flapped open and closed as he tried to breathe, and a split-second later, every part of him fell loose and hung limply, like he was nothing more than a dangling marionette. Uncontrolled, dead.

Mom screamed. The giant tossed Dad's lifeless body into the snow and started marching toward the wagon.

Nikka did the only thing she could think of. She crawled across the wagon and dropped into the front seat. She picked up the reins and gave them a snap.

"Go!" she screamed at the two horses. She snapped the reins again, but they didn't move.

The snow crunched under the giant's enormous feet. He drew a knife from his belt as he walked toward the wagon.

"Go, you bastards!" Nikka pleaded with the horses.

It was then that she noticed the horses were not horses at all. They were life-size stuffed animals. They had shiny, black button eyes and fuzzy cloth for fur.

Mom howled as the giant took her by the throat and raised her high. He didn't wait for Mom to fight back. He slid his blade slowly into her gut and walked it up her abdomen with a crooked expression that could have been a smile on a shadowy monster like him.

She screamed. She cried. Her tone turned to gurgles as the knife reached her ribs and dug up into her lungs.

"Mom!" it was all Nikka could get out. Tears rushed over her cheeks and froze on her chin. There was nothing she could do to save her mother, and she knew it. All she could do now was try to save herself.

Nikka turned away, readying herself to drop to the other side of the wagon. She jumped, and there was a thud as something slammed her from behind.

It pushed her forward, down into the snow. Her face was instantly frozen as she hit the ground. Her back was wet and hot.

No. It can't be. What was behind her couldn't have been what she thought it was.

Nikka crawled and turned, desperate to get out from under whatever was on top of her. Then she saw what it was: Mom.

Her mother stared into her eyes. She was dead, Nikka could see that, but her gaze looked right into Nikka's and her insides spilled onto her child as Nikka scrambled to get out from under her.

There was a crunch in the snow. The giant was coming around.

There was a crackle in the woods. Something was clawing at the underbrush beyond the trees. Branches snapped, and the ground shook.

Nikka slipped from below her mother, her skin crawling at the brush of slick entrails that caressed her escape. She leaped to her feet. She took a single step, and something hooked her foot and yanked her back. She was lifted into the air upside down, and she saw him clearly. She saw the dark face of evil. It had come from that cabin with nothing in mind except to kill. It had done it to Dad and then Mom, and now it had her. She didn't know what he wanted after that, but she had the strangest vision of a Lucky Shot Burger as he raised his knife.

"No!" she howled at him.

She could have sworn he was chuckling to himself as tears raced from her eyes into her hair, as she saw Mom on the ground behind him, her body crumpled, limbs bent, crooked and red.

The thing in the woods crashed through the trees. An enormous bug leg plunged into the giant's thigh and dragged him to the ground. The giant released Nikka and stabbed the beast. Nikka slapped against the snow and felt something hard and sharp, a broken branch or a stump, stab her in the palm.

The giant roared and knifed the bug in the face. The bug used another limb and ripped into the giant's leg.

Nikka had no idea what was happening, but she wasn't going to sit there and watch. She climbed to her feet, leaking a trail of blood from her hand. She ran up the wagon trail through the snow as the giant screamed from behind her.

She didn't mean to, but she turned and looked as she ran. The man hung in three pieces from three different insect legs. Nikka had hope as she looked forward again, but that all dropped away when another bug stabbed her in the gut and lifted her into the air.

Nikka gasped as she opened her eyes inside the tent. The nylon roof was lighter than she last remembered. Was morning coming?

She reached for her phone to check the time, and her hand ached.

"Shit."

It was 5:11 a.m., and in the light of her flashlight, she saw a scar on her palm where she had cut her hand in her dream.

"No." She shook her head. She couldn't believe that. She had been having terrifying nightmares forever, and they had never physically hurt her. "It doesn't make sense." She looked her hand over again and again.

It didn't matter. It was time to get ready for the day. Once she was at Masha's and took the next dose, everything would be okay for the next week. She just needed to focus and get there. She had to believe that.

So focus was what Nikka did.

She sat up and prepared her mind for the day. She didn't want to leave yet; better to wait for the sun if she didn't intend to bump into nocturnal predators on their final hunt of the night. So she went through her bag. She ate. She dressed. She thought of positive things, projecting them into her future.

Dose two of five was coming. The world was good, full of possibilities.

It was going to be bright and open, and she would have joy when this was all over.

When the sun's morning rays twinkled on the side of the tent, Nikka finally ventured out. She rolled up her sleeping bag and packed her tent, cursing at how hard it was to make them as compact as the lady in the store had, and then she attached them both to her bag.

She was on her way.

She reached the fork and turned toward Rocky Bottom; she reached the stream and followed it.

Throughout the entire walk, Nikka refused to think about her dreams. Not the cabin in the woods or the snowstorm or the giant or the bug-men. She refused to look at her palm.

She watched the trees instead.

The swaying boughs in the heights of the forest moved with an almost metronomic rhythm, like there was a song to the forest that only they could hear. The sun rose higher and shone through the needles with a glimmer that reminded her of a diamond, of the way she used to be amazed when sunlight gleamed and scattered through her mother's engagement ring and tiny rainbow-rimmed dots danced on the ceiling. The babble of the water in Rocky Bottom soothed her ears; it whispered that she was awake now and had nothing to fear from a long-gone dream.

It all added up to a mellowing sensation, a sign of the approach of Black Creek.

She could feel Masha as she moved closer to the creek. There were layers in that feeling, and for some reason, she didn't dare dig below the first. That one was warm and welcoming. The Masha from her first dream was there, the one that felt like an old friend who was only there to help. It was reminiscent of her grandmother in a way, a woman from the old country that she only saw once when she was very small, but the woman had been full of a softened comfort and deep joy.

She ignored the sour, stinging taste below this feeling. It had a dark, clawing hunger that she couldn't quite pinpoint and wouldn't investigate. It was something that was trying to hide, like the tartness of milk that was about to sour, and Nikka was happy to let it remain unseen.

When she set foot on the bank of Black Creek, her heart raced. Her pace picked up. She needed what was ahead. It was freedom, true freedom to be herself and live her life. It was a release from the shackles of her unconscious mind and a doorway to her future. She would do whatever it took to grab it with both hands and hold tight.

Nikka paused when she reached the sitting log. It was different than last week. Not a lot; it was something she may not have noticed if her heart wasn't pounding and her mind wasn't taking in every spec and glimmer.

The log was older. Mold and moss trimmed the edges. It wasn't something she would have called rotten, but it was different than last time—*wasn't it?*

She pondered this. Maybe she just hadn't noticed last time? She had been sleep-deprived, practically sleepwalking. Could she really gauge whether what she witnessed last time as accurate?

Nikka looked at the tiny shack. It was trimmed with the same green edges as the log, the start of mold, the tiny hairs of moss sprouting from cracks in the wood, and the gentle grasses that had been on the roof had turned brown. The festooned vines around the corners had lost their flowers, and the entire thing seemed somehow sad.

She had to have just overlooked these things before. Again, she had been sleep-deprived, almost in a dream as she got there. Yes, her memory of the place was of it being immaculate and new, but that was probably just how it felt as a result of her exhaustion and hope.

And none of this mattered. What mattered was inside and waiting: Masha and Nikka's next dose.

She walked to the door, raising her closed hand to knock, and Masha answered the second her knuckles rapped.

"Come, come." Masha's voice was enchanting.

Nikka's heart skipped a beat. There was an instant where fear ran through her veins, a coldness that shouted *RUN!*—it was immediately doused by a wash of heat from the door and an irresistible urge to cross the threshold. So she did.

Chapter Eleven

Nikka's gaze shot straight toward Masha, at the tiny stove, at the simmering pot that she was sure held her next dose.

"So early today?" Masha stirred the pot.

Nikka grinned as she stepped inside and closed the door behind her. She moved across the tiny home, and Masha raised a hand.

"Take off your bag. Relax."

"Yeah." Nikka had forgotten she was even wearing it. She was so excited to get to Masha's potion. She slid the pack off her shoulders and set it on the floor.

"You spent the night in the woods. That was brave."

"Was it?" People hiked and camped in the forest all the time—didn't they? Nikka looked up at Masha, who somehow looked older as she swayed, stirring the concoction with a slow swooping pace.

"It's springtime. All the forest creatures are especially hungry this time of year." Her jet-black hair was not quite as black. Streaks of gray hung like stiff, frayed wires in her dangling locks. Crow's-feet bunched around her eyes, and her knuckles seemed somehow more pronounced on her digits as they gripped her long wooden stirring spoon.

But her eyes, they stared at Nikka with a cold strength that warned her this woman was as quick and dangerous as a young viper—only as Nikka blinked, Masha's smile overtook every detail she had observed. Masha was there to help her, after all. Masha was her friend, and the love of friendship was warm between them, filling Nikka from her chest to her extremities.

"I guess I didn't think about that," Nikka said as she leaned toward the pot, toward her salvation.

"A young woman like you must always be careful. There are so many predators in this world." Masha pointed at the tiny table. "Sit. It will be a couple more minutes."

"Oh." Nikka didn't want to wait. She wanted the dose now. She tried not to let the disappointment show on her face because she knew she was being over-eager. There was a miracle happening here; you shouldn't expect a miracle worker to rush just for you.

She turned toward the table and felt a prick on the back of her neck. Then it was hot. It was like something had bitten her. She covered her neck with her fingers expecting to smash a mosquito but felt nothing.

"Just a few more minutes." Masha stirred and flicked her fingers over the pot. Her necklace seemed to hover over the brew, its dark crystals the length of fingers hung from the chain, and as Nikka watched it sway, it mesmerized her. Were the crystals glowing?

"How was your week?" the witch asked. "Your tasks weren't too difficult, I assume."

Nikka had put those out of her mind, especially the creepier parts—the totes that shifted around with the sound of wetness. That was almost a week ago, and she was happy not to think about it. But as Masha mentioned the tasks, Nikka remembered this was an exchange—she had to work for this dose. She would have more jobs to do for Masha this week.

She didn't want to do more jobs like those, but she would.

"They weren't too bad." She shivered.

"Good." Masha smiled. "My friends need more help this week."

Nikka knew it. "O-okay."

"So you're still willing to help? To take on the tasks in exchange for your next dose?"

"Yes." Nikka nodded with her entire body. She was sure.

"Good. Because at this point, if you stopped taking the doses before the sequence was complete, there could be... side effects."

"What kind of side effects?"

Masha raised a cup and scooped from her pot with a ladle. Liquid ran into the cup, and as Nikka watched her cure pour—it was coming, *Yes!*—she completely forgot about her question.

"Here you go, dear." Masha crossed the room. The cup in her hand was steaming, and Nikka's mouth watered for it.

She took the cup in both of her hands and raised it to her lips. Shivers ran down her body, and her muscles tensed from her feet to her face. This was it; this was going to bring her one step closer to freedom.

Tears burned the corners of her eyes as the cup touched her lips and the tastes of vegetation, spice, and metals slipped over her tongue and the thick liquid ran down her throat. It cooled her chest and her belly. It spread through her nerves and her veins. The coldness was gripping as it ran through her core to her limbs and her brain.

She trembled and closed her eyes, embracing the feeling. It wasn't a good feeling, not any of it, but it was symbolic in her mind. It was a passage she was traveling through that would take her where she wanted to go.

When it was all down and Nikka opened her eyes, she wanted to scream. Her brain flooded with fear. Her eyes shifted around, taking in the place, but Nikka was frozen beyond that.

What she saw she could only describe as Hell. The shack dripped with blood. Bodies that should have been dead—they had no skin—writhed and clawed at each other. Creatures crawled across the ceiling and walls, black things with too many legs, layered in blood, and something that could have been Masha but looked more like a thousand years old than thirty or forty stood in front of Nikka. Watching Nikka. Grinning at Nikka with wide, gray lips, blackened yellow teeth, and eyes that were dripping black—pure black.

Nikka closed her eyes and held them that way.

There was no way what she had just seen was real. She remembered last time she took the drink she saw things. That had to have been what this was. It was some *side effect* of the magic soaking into her system.

Reluctantly, Nikka opened her eyes.

"There you are," Masha said.

The room was back to normal... or, mostly so. Nikka noticed cracks in the table, rough edges that had seemed smooth last week. The walls of the shack were similarly changed, wood that seemed to have aged ten years since she was there last.

But none of that mattered. Like the moss or Masha's gray hairs, those things didn't matter. All that mattered was that the potion worked. She felt the coolness fade from her body, but she knew it was in there. It would work.

She smiled.

"There you go." Masha gently took the cup from Nikka's hand. "I can tell; it's working already."

It was, wasn't it?

Nikka could feel her mind calming. She could feel the thoughts of bug monsters falling away like they were sinking into a well.

"Will it be better this week?" Nikka asked. "I mean, my dreams were so much better last week—I just mean, they always came back at the end."

"Maybe," Masha said. "It's still early. You're not even halfway through. But I think if you work hard and complete your tasks, there's a good chance you may not see your demons at all this week."

Nikka trembled at the idea. She imagined sleeping through the night, waking the next day, and not having seen them once.

Her palm itched. The scar.

She looked at it and showed Masha. "Is this part of it?"

Masha took Nikka's hand in hers. She squinted as she examined the scar. "This is not mine. There are hungry things in those woods beyond the Rocky Bottom."

Nikka took back her hand. "I'll get home then."

"Yes. Get home and rest. Your tasks begin again tomorrow."

Nikka didn't know how many times she thanked Masha as she put on her pack and left. It was sincere, and it was out of worry that if she wasn't sincere, Masha could find someone else to do her jobs. She had to keep Masha happy.

She didn't look at the house or the sitting log as she left. The saying hung in her mind: *You never look a gift horse in the mouth.*

She hurried along the creek, along Rocky Bottom, down the path, and back to her car. She tossed the bag in the back and collapsed in the driver's seat.

She couldn't stop herself from bursting into laughter. This whole thing was so absurd. Her dreams, the witch, her *tasks,* even the scar on her hand. None of it made sense, and she was happily going along with it all.

She laughed so hard it hurt her belly and her ears.

But she had swallowed two out of five doses. She was getting closer.

She started the car and headed home, stopping by Lucky Shot Burger on the way.

Nikka was so hungry she ate her burger on the drive. It was nothing more than a balled-up wrapper when she walked in the door and crashed on the couch. She set it on the coffee table with the others.

She was creating quite a collection there. She knew she needed to straighten the place up, that Rich and Lynn would probably be upset to come home and find the growing mess, but that thought quickly slipped from her mind as she picked up the remote and started scrolling through her options.

Nikka had homework to do for tomorrow's class. She needed to start thinking about finding a new job. She didn't want to live off her savings if she didn't have to. But all of those concerns were shallow compared to her need to relax. She had a good dream coming, she was sure of it, and that was more important than any of that other stuff, especially after her shitty night in that tent.

She pushed the night in the tent out of her mind. She didn't want to weigh the implications of a dream that left her with a scar or whatever animals were out there. Her doses would fix it all, and she wasn't going to do that again.

Nikka settled on *Rosanne,* a show her dad used to watch. She found herself drawn more and more to things that reminded her of Mom and Dad lately, now that she was dreaming about them and allowing herself to think about them more often.

It started, and before the opening credits were done, she was asleep and sitting in a chair in the Conners's kitchen.

Nikka yawned and stretched on the couch. It was mid-afternoon and she had slept through a dozen episodes of the Connor's shenanigans before her app stopped and the TV went into screensaver mode. Looking at the afternoon shadows through the curtains and the TV and the balls of burger remains on the table, she realized she was smiling.

She had slept—slept a long time—and she hadn't seen a single insect bastard. She hadn't awakened with a start. She wasn't panting and sweating.

The second dose had worked!

"Jesus, it worked."

She cried where she sat and looked at the ceiling as if she could see all the way to Heaven and imagined Mom and Dad looking down. They would have been so happy for her.

She let it sink in for a little while before she rose to go to her room and work on her homework. As she glanced past her room, up the darkened hallway, past the bathroom and Rich and Lynn's room, she noticed a strange thing in the shadows, and she had to stop and look at it.

Beyond her roommate's door, in the darkest part of the hall, was a shape. Nikka imagined that seeing a shape there at any other time in the past few years would have sent her screaming and crying into her room to hide under the covers. Today, though, was different.

She knew it wasn't really a person, though it reminded her of one. It made her think of the girl from her dream the other day—on the beach with Mom and Dad in that scene from *Lost*—Lillian. Lilly, who had brought her Lucky Shot Burger and had been in her class so many years ago.

It was odd to see a shadowy shape like that in this hallway, and while it did give her a freezing sensation behind her belly, much like the one from her earlier dose, she decided to ignore it.

It wasn't really Lilly. It couldn't have been. It was just her brain working to wake itself up and forming familiar shapes out of random darkness.

It was still a little chilling, and it made her wonder what Lilly was up to as she went into her room and sat at her desk.

She put on her headphones and started to work. She didn't hear the footfalls in the hallway.

Chapter Twelve

L ILLY WATCHED AS NIKKA went into her room and shut the door behind her. She thought for sure the girl was going to say something, to confront her for being in the apartment—Nikka looked right at her, she had to have seen her—but she didn't.

Lilly shrugged and walked toward the kitchen.

She had already searched through the roommate's room and found nothing interesting. There was a TV and a pair of tablets, but she wasn't there for those. There was a wallet with a few bucks in it, and she took the money—the guy was dead, after all, he didn't need it. There were some nice pieces of jewelry the girl had left behind. She could have been interested in those if she was still using, but just like the tablets, she left them where they were.

She walked into the kitchen wondering what she might find. There was a tingling sensation in her gut telling her there was something good in there.

The counters were a mess. Trash everywhere. Sink filled with dirty plates and mugs. That was close to what she was expecting after the mess in the living room. She hadn't looked too carefully at it when she came in; she just snuck past the sleeping girl on the couch and headed straight back.

She got a rush when sneaking through other people's homes, one she always enjoyed. Since she was fifteen and robbing houses with Adrian to pay for their habits, she loved it. The adrenaline kick was almost better than the reward, and she would have kept doing it even without the drugs.

And so, it was different now.

She didn't need to rob anyone for drug money, the addiction was fading with each job and each time she puked. She was in that apartment today because of curiosity... and something more that she wasn't quite sure of.

She had been inside each house and apartment of her victims since the witch put her on that mission. It was something she was compelled to do. She had their keys, wallets, and IDs, so she had to know what they were like in life. She had to go to these places and feel them. So she did the same with Rich and Lynn.

She expected the place to be cleaner, though. Lynn had this real aura of a tight-ass clean freak. But as Lilly looked around, she decided this was all from the roommate she had just seen, a roommate that looked so familiar she had to know her.

Lilly opened the fridge. Just the thought of eating made her stomach lurch, but the curiosity forced her—something else too.

There had to be a dozen balled-up wrappers from Lucky Shot Burger in there, most the size of just a bite or two, like someone was saving the last swallow of their burger for later.

Her stomach gurgled. It was exactly the same as her refrigerator. It was more like she had opened a portal to her own fridge than the door in some random apartment.

She picked one up without thinking. She unwrapped it, and the smell of cold meat, cheese, ketchup, and mustard was too much. She crammed it into her mouth. Her eyes pinched shut. She savored the meat, and even though she knew what would happen next, she couldn't stop herself.

It went down her throat, and she balled up the wrapper. She tossed it on the counter and perched over the sink.

The second the chewed-up bite reached her stomach, it reversed, pushed up by acids and her cramping abdomen. She puked over the dirty plates and dishes, the familiar burn like a hated friend she couldn't avoid.

Every bit of ground beef, cheese, and bun hit the dishes, and her body lurched again. Pain and cramping, hot bile up her throat and over her lips. It was already all out, but her body didn't care. It was the ritual. It had to happen.

She coughed, and her eyes bulged. Her head felt swollen and ready to pop, and no sooner than she was able to suck in half a breath it happened again. A retch of only bile as her body convulsed and cramped. Tears came, and she was sure she was going to hack up her stomach itself, and it all happened again.

With her mouth dripping stringy spit, Lilly's eyes filled with white and black dots. Her legs went limp below her, and she dropped, slamming her chin on the sink before her ass slapped the tile floor.

She caught herself there, getting her hands below her before she went all the way down. She could barely see the kitchen through the haze of specs, and her chin was hot—she wondered if she had split it open, and she actually wanted to laugh at how stupid she had been.

Adrian never forgot how stupid she could be, and though she was glad to be rid of him, there were things she missed. For example, he was the only one he allowed to put her down. When they were camped out in the abandoned house on West Hemlock before it burned down, there had been two other guys with them: Frankie and Bricks.

Frankie looked at Lilly every day, up and down, and she knew that if she was ever left alone with him, something bad would happen. Bricks wasn't that bad. He was practically brain-dead from all the meth he had smoked, and Lilly didn't think he could even remember his real name anymore after how severely he had fried his mind, but he never struck

Lilly as dangerous, not like Frankie.

The thing that stuck out to Lilly, the reason she was even thinking about Adrian and Frankie and Bricks, was the specks in her vision.

The house couldn't have been vacant for more than a few weeks when they claimed it. It was in a nice neighborhood, and they knew they only had a matter of time before someone took over ownership, even with all the deaths and the bloodstains soaking the floors and walls. It seemed like there was always some asshole willing to flip a house, no matter what state it was in. No matter how much death and blood had been spilled there. So Lilly knew they only had a while to squat there, but with the snowy autumn outside and the dope in their veins most of the time, they were okay with a temporary place, even one caked in blood.

It was about two weeks later when it happened. Bricks and Frankie both had taken rooms on the second floor, and Lilly and Adrian had taken the top. It was the middle of the night, and the house was quiet except for the weird noises that never seemed to stop, the ones that sounded like whispers that even when Lilly was high and put her fingers in her ears she couldn't stop from hearing.

Bricks was asleep in his room. Frankie was supposedly in his. Adrian had been feeling horny and made Lilly ride him, and though the door to that room never really shut, Lilly was pretty sure it had spread open more than a crack while she was on top. She had felt eyes on her, too, though she always felt that in that damned house.

When Adrian was done and yanked her off, he rolled over and passed out. Lilly was nowhere near done, but it was what it was, and with the house's temperature dropping as the night moved deeper, all she wanted then was to curl up under the thin scratchy blanket she had found in the closet and sleep. She was almost there when she felt something messing with her hands.

Lilly opened her eyes and saw Frankie. He was hovering over her, tying the last knot to keep her wrists together. She opened her mouth to scream and felt the gag. She was going to do it anyway, and his fist crashed into her temple.

She saw the spots as he covered his lips with his finger and hissed, "Shhhh."

Adrian snored. He might as well have been on another planet.

Frankie grabbed Lilly's ankles and dragged her.

The cold night stung her uncovered legs and bare arms, and the floor scratched her skin as she thumped from the grimy mattress onto the rough wood planks. She felt it all through a dizzying haze. Her heart thudded as she prayed to escape. She knew what was going to happen. It wasn't the first time in her short life she had been threatened with rape.

Lilly was on the edge of the steps, and he went back and closed the door. She shifted her weight, leaning forward, hoping to slide down the stairs on her rear, hoping to get some distance between herself and Frankie.

It didn't go how she planned.

Her butt slipped calmly from the first step to the second. As she descended to the next, Frankie turned and saw her moving. He darted toward her, and she pushed herself downward.

"Bitch!" he hissed.

She slid down two steps at once, and there was no more control in her descent. It was too fast, and as she tried to slow herself with her foot, it caught on a step and rolled under her. There was a ripping sound and pain as it bent backward and under her rear, and Lilly toppled face-first over the next two steps and slammed into the landing.

More stars in her vision. Her entire face was on fire from the impact, and blood streamed from her mouth. She would have cried, but it hurt to move anything.

"You fucking bitch." Frankie came down after her. His fists were tight.

"You want the pain, don't you?" He shook his head and seized her legs.

"No," Lilly whimpered through her gag. She was already in pain. She didn't want more. She wanted it to stop. She wanted to be somewhere else and get high, drift far away from this place on a cloud of meth and never look back.

Frankie held her in place and lifted her shirt, exposing her naked ass. Was he going to do it right here on the stairs? He wrestled with his pants, and she tried to move. He punched her in the back of the head.

When Lilly opened her eyes, Adrian was dragging Frankie down the steps. She couldn't see clearly just then, but Frankie's face was definitely red. When they reached the next set of stairs, Adrian stood Frankie up, wound back his fist, and punched Frankie so hard in the face Lilly could hear his nose shatter.

Blood streamed through the air as Frankie fell back onto the next flight of stairs, crumpling and rolling like a child's toy.

Adrian picked Lilly up in his arms and carried her back upstairs to that disgusting mattress. He set her down gently, unbound her, and covered her with the blanket.

They lay peacefully with each other the rest of that night, lovingly, in a way Lilly remembered happening fewer times than she had fingers to count, and regrettably, it was a fond memory she held onto each time he hurt her as if those occasions made the others worth it. She would do that until she met the witch.

She didn't see Frankie again.

She wondered what had ever happened to Frankie as her vision cleared and she sat on Rich and Lynn's kitchen floor. She wondered if she could find him, make use of him the way she had the others, the way she had Adrian. She would have liked that.

Lilly stood. She took a step toward the bedroom the girl had gone into. As she neared the door, there was a pull. There was something about that girl that made her want to know more. She had wondered about taking her, chopping her up like she had the roommate, but that thought now seemed repulsive. She wanted instead to talk to the girl.

But you don't just walk into someone's room and say *Hi*. She would find another way.

Still, she couldn't leave just yet. She stood in the hallway by the bedroom door, her ear almost touching the wood. She heard music playing and the clack of fingers on a keyboard. She felt warmth through the door, a welcoming sensation like when she first met the witch. That had been nice, regardless of how sickly she felt right at that second.

There was a draw here, and she needed to know more.

Tomorrow, she thought. After her next job, after she was cleaned up and didn't smell like rot or puke. Then she would see what this was about.

On the way to the front door, Lilly drooled at the balled-up Lucky Shot Burger wrappers on the coffee table. She was hungry. God, she was so hungry.

But it was almost over. Just a couple more weeks. She could see the bodies between herself and the end, and though the mound was growing, she would climb to the top, and she would succeed.

Chapter Thirteen

Nikka had barely opened her eyes when she felt the urge. It was dark out still; she could see there was no orange glow of sunrise around her window.

Why so early?

She would have never thought she would be lamenting the loss of sleep, but here she was, lying in bed knowing that it was time to get up and do her job... and she wanted to close her eyes and sleep.

She laughed and threw back the covers. Her phone said it was 4:35 a.m.

She laughed again and stretched. She pulled on a pair of jeans from the floor by the end of the bed that she had no idea if they were clean or not, a bra hanging from her desk chair, and the first shirt her fingers found inside her top drawer. On the way from her room, she grabbed a hoodie from the hook on the back of her bedroom door.

Nikka made her coffee quickly. With ten times more experience than most women her age, she had a single cup poured into her travel mug with sugar and creamer in barely longer than it took to put on her shoes and tie them. A few minutes later, she was in her car and driving... somewhere.

The streets of Custer Falls were mostly empty that early in the morning. Nikka passed a car or two as she drove east and then north, and finally stopped in the desolate parking lot of a small church she didn't recognize.

There was a point, a tall steeple at the top of the building, and that surprised Nikka. Most modern churches, she thought, were going for a more contemporary feel, buildings that looked more like stores or warehouses than traditional churches. Not that she was particularly religious, but she kind of admired the boldness of the idea. *Let people know what you are and be proud of it.* It reminded her of a church she would have expected in some southern town a hundred years ago, and images of Tom Sawyer and Huckleberry Finn ducking from responsibilities and fleeing to the river rang in her mind.

She drove around to the back of the building and pulled up beside a van at a set of stairs leading to the back door. This was where she was supposed to park, she just knew that. She also knew she was supposed to go inside.

Inside?

The fact that a witch would send her inside a church seemed odd on its face, but it felt completely natural. There was a job in there for her to do.

She turned off the car and headed up the stairs to a white door with a single vertical window. She knocked once, and a man's face appeared in the glass. He was middle-aged, with gray-streaked black hair and a mustache that matched. He wore glasses that seemed a little too big for his face, and his expression was somewhere between relieved and excited when he set eyes on her.

There was a click, and the door was unlocked and opened. He held out his hand. "Come on in. I'm Pastor Sanders, but you can call me Jules."

Nikka shook his hand. It was surprisingly warm.

"I'm Nikki," she said.

"This way." He backed into the hallway, a steel-walled room with shelves of cleaners, snow melt, and other custodial equipment. She followed, and he led her through a pair of doors, down a short hallway, and into a cathedral-roofed sanctuary, the heart of the church.

The pews were dark, stained oak, as were the open trusses and beams above and the enormous cross hanging behind the pulpit. It wasn't quite what she would call flashy, but it was definitely bold, a place built with love and dedication.

"You're new, right?" Nikka was following him blindly now. She spotted the stained glass on the sides of the building, each depicting a different scene she imaged was from an apostle's life. Each seemed off in a way she couldn't put her finger on.

"Yes, just opened up, actually. We've been blessed to already be building a small congregation. I'd give a lot of the credit to Youth Pastor Salas, who spends a lot of time on TikTok." He stopped at the last pew, turned, and faced her. "It really is wonderful, especially after our original build site collapsed into the ground."

That made her turn. She had heard about the accident on 10th Avenue where the ground collapsed into some kind of underground cave system. "That was your construction site?"

"That was us." He gestured up at the building. "But God found us a new home, and here we are."

"Okay." A shiver went down Nikka's spine. She wasn't quite sure why other than, for some reason, talking to the deeply religious always seemed to push her back a little. She didn't mind faith; she thought people should believe what they wanted to, but such strong conviction, the absence of doubt, was something she didn't quite get. She wasn't even sure that people had been to the moon, or why some days felt sadder than others, or if the next time she flipped the switch the light in the kitchen would come on. That fact that someone could be so sure about the creator of the universe—of everything—was mind-boggling to her.

"He's here." The pastor gestured at the last pew.

Nikka felt a sudden tremble at those words. She thought they were the only two people in the hall, and then her eyes ran across the pew. Gazing at the roof and the windows and everything else, she had completely overlooked the dead old man lying on the back bench.

He wore layers of ragged clothes: jackets, jeans, and even shoes with holes. His hair was frazzled and thin, gray and oily. One arm hung from the pew, almost touching the floor, and the other was stationary on his chest as if holding his heart, praying it wasn't a heart attack or his last moment on Earth.

"Him?" Nikka pointed.

"I think the two of us will be enough. I can get his arms if you want to carry from his feet."

His feet? She was carrying a dead old man today? *What the fuck?*

She wanted to back away, to turn right there and run. She couldn't carry a dead guy. She flashed with images of totes in the back of her car. She didn't know what was in there—not for sure—but she had a few guesses. But those were covered. She was allowed to imagine they weren't what she thought they were. She was allowed to lie about what she thought they were.

This was different.

She shook her head, and as if answering her hesitation, a scene popped into her mind: insects in a warehouse, as big as elephants, ripping her to pieces. The nightmares. The never-ending waves of exhaustion. The knowledge that she couldn't live that way, and one way or another, her life with those nightmares couldn't last much longer.

She had to do this. It was the deal.

Besides, he's already dead.

"I'll get the feet," she agreed.

"Good." Pastor Sanders stepped beside the man and took hold of his dead hands. He watched and waited as Nikka hesitantly gripped the feet. He nodded, and they lifted.

The old guy was heavier than she expected. It took a lot for her to carry her end as the pastor led them back to the rear of the church and through the hallway.

Her heart thudded. She didn't think she had ever touched a dead body, let alone carried one. It didn't seem real, but the adrenaline in her veins did. It kept her fully aware that this whole thing could send her to jail if she got caught. She wasn't sure the charge, but whatever she was a part of had to be illegal.

They set the body down beside the door, and the holy man peeked outside to be sure the coast was clear. He gave Nikka another nod. She didn't like it; it was too cheery for this type of thing, for a supposedly religious man physically handling a dead body.

Pastor Sanders pushed the door with his back and led them to the car. They had to put the man down again while Nikka dug out her keys.

She couldn't help but look into the old man's blank eyes as she searched for them. She found them with sweaty hands, and his face struck her as a kind one, a gentle old man who could have been a grand-father, a war vet, a neighbor. His eyes stared into the dark sky with false dawn rising, and the idea that she was manipulating his corpse made her sick. It made her skin crawl.

She had to close her eyes and breathe to recenter herself.

"Are you okay, child?" the pastor asked. There was a slickness to it, something that made Nikka feel that he wanted to take her back to his office and mistakenly feel her up under the guise of consoling her.

"Yeah." She unlocked the rear hatch and lifted it. She didn't look at the pastor, just took the feet and waited.

Pastor Sanders lifted the old man, and they set him into the rear of the car. It occurred to Nikka that the body wasn't as well disguised as the totes had been, and she grabbed a loose blanket from her backseat and spread it over the old man.

"Good thinking," the holy man said.

She shut the rear.

"Thank you for your help," the pastor said, and held out his hand for her to take.

Nikka was surprised he had all of his fingers.

He rolled his eyes as if remembering and pulled back his hand. "I almost forgot." He reached into his slacks, and Nikka squinted as she watched him.

What was he doing?

He brought out a knife.

Nikka stepped back.

The pastor held his hand against the railing of the church's back stairs, and with his other, he sawed into his hand. His face remained focused on the act. He didn't flinch or scowl in pain. He guided his knife around his knuckle, through his tendons, and between the bones.

She thought he smiled when he was done, admiring his accomplishment.

Pastor Sanders slid the knife back into his pocket and held out a warm, severed finger for Nikka to take. No Baggie. No subterfuge. As clear in the light of the coming dawn as everything else around them. "Can't forget this."

The only way she stopped herself from puking was by clenching her lips tight. She extended her hand and took the digit between her thumb and index finger. It dripped blood onto the pavement.

He grinned, cocked his head, and said, "Goodbye, then. See you next time."

Prickles ran all over her, dragged down her body like a thousand frozen spiders. *Next time? God, please, let me not have to ever come back here.*

He turned and strolled back inside. She watched him, letting the finger drip and hoping not to get any of it on her. She was still standing in the same place when the door clicked shut.

She contained herself until she reached the driver's door, where she let the puke go.

<hr>

With the rear shut and the finger in an empty, disposable coffee cup Nikka found in her cup holder, she was back on the road. She shivered and wanted so badly to pull over at the Wesker Pump and grab something to wash away the puke taste from her mouth. But she just couldn't take that chance with the dead old man in the rear.

Nikka found herself back on the west side of town, following nothing but her gut. She was back in that instinctual zone where she was sure it was Masha silently guiding her, and before she knew it, she was at Ramon and Sons Funeral home once again.

She chuckled to herself. She should have expected that, shouldn't she? She had a dead guy—where do dead guys go?

She drove around the back, and there he was, Mr. Ramon. He stood beside a gurney.

He didn't have to tell her. She turned the car around and backed up toward him. When she was out of the car and walking to the rear, he was grinning at her. His bandaged hand was pure white this time, no bloody leaks.

What a sick fuck.

She opened the car. "Here you go."

She didn't have to tell him twice. He peeled back the blanket and looked the old man over, but just for a second.

Nikka couldn't help but think she would have rather Mr. Ramon left the blanket on—and taken it. She didn't expect she would ever use that thing again. Whether there was a drop of anything from the dead guy on it or not, it was contaminated now, and in a way that no washing could fix.

Ramon leaned forward, using his arms like a forklift, and scooped up the old guy. He set him down gently on the gurney with a practiced level of respect.

Nikka was somewhat surprised. After last time, she figured the guy would just throw the old man like a sack.

She shut the hatch and turned to leave, and Mr. Ramon said, "Can you give me a hand for just a second?"

Nikka felt a squirming sensation under her skin. Whatever this guy wanted, she didn't want to be a part of it. She searched inside herself, trying to understand if there was a push one way or the other from Masha. Was this a part of the task? Or was it just the weird mortician asking for something extra?

"Just for a second," he said. He must have seen the conflict on her face. "I just need a hand getting him into the embalming room."

That seemed weird. Wasn't he used to doing this all by himself? Didn't funeral homes have specialized equipment to facilitate one person...

She hadn't found an answer from Masha, but she decided she should do it. The last thing she needed was to fail at a task and make Masha mad.

"Yeah." It seemed like as soon as she agreed, the smell from inside found her.

He grinned. "Just push from that side. I'll lead the way." He did. Up the ramp and through the doors.

A wave of stench flooded Nikka. It was worse than last time. There was a deep odor of decay, of moist dead things that she didn't think was supposed to be there. She imagined some bodies smelled when they got to a place like this, but wasn't Mr. Ramon's job to clean them out and stop it? To *sanitize* death for his clients? She thought that was why embalming existed.

They were starting down the hall toward the preparation room when Nikka noticed the room to the left. The door was open, and the smell was so bad she could feel it staining her body from just being present. It looked like it was a storage room, but lining the floors were trash bags, full trash bags whose shapes didn't make sense. While most were on their sides, piled or leaning in a way that made them look like amorphous blobs, several held distinct forms that Nikka couldn't unsee. They stood against the wall or leaned on others with round, head-shaped tops. Their lower portions were unmistakably human—or pieces thereof—the mid-sections of corpses.

They were bagged people with no arms or legs, and they sat in that room rotting. They decomposed in the back space of a place that was supposed to respect them and prepare them for eternal rest.

The smell exposed more than Nikka wanted to face. It was like she could see within those bags. She could see the skin turning pale and the insides liquefying as internal acids melted through organs and leaked and bacteria broke down solid structures, tuning them to mush. They were melting in those bags, and she could picture it all.

She could see the invaders.

There were living things in there, digging things. There were maggots eating the rotting tissues. There were worms running through it all, slurping and slithering. They were growing and plumping in that masses of viscera.

She saw it all in a second, and in the one that followed, she saw where those maggots and worms led: to the things in her dreams, to the monsters she saw in Sully's backyard, to the enormous bug creatures.

Her body went numb, and her fingers went limp. The gurney seemed to vanish from her grip, and the room went dark.

Chapter Fourteen

T HEY WERE ALL AROUND her. Bug after bug, an army of them.

Nikka was on the log by the creek, and they encircled her, twenty feet away and coming toward her from every angle. Their legs thumped as the tips of their massive limbs stabbed the dirt, stabbed the mud, splashed in the shallow water. Tiny earthquakes shook the ground as they moved ever closer. The air came on thick with the scents of death and hunger.

They were locked on to her, and she knew it was going to be like it had been before the witch. They were going to stab her and rip her apart. They would devour her despite what she was told and the potion and the tasks. It was going to be like so many times before—maybe even worse.

She screamed. There was nothing else she could do. It was out of pure panic, out of knowing how bad it was going to hurt and that she had no other defense inside her.

It only seemed to energize them. There was a clattering sound as their mandibles rubbed together in eagerness, in anticipation of the meal to come. Nikka could feel a buzz in the air. They hadn't had her in days, and they were starving.

A whistle cut through the noise as one of the beasts darted forward and its claw-tipped leg flew at Nikka.

She saw it descending toward her foot, and time slowed. It was like the thing's dirty sharpened claw was shining in the dim forest, and that shine was full of glee. It wanted to slice and stab. It wanted to taste her blood and to rip and tear.

She didn't know where it came from, but something inside her at that moment said *No*.

Nikka pulled her foot back as hard and as fast as she could. It didn't cut the air as that claw did, but it was quick—though not quite quick enough.

The leg came down, its tip stabbing into Nikka's shoe. It sliced through leather and rubber, and she felt searing pain as it cut the sole of her foot.

She opened her mouth to scream, but as she did, that voice repeated *No*.

The scream that came out was not one of pain or terror. Nikka surprised herself as the scream ripped from her throat as a wall of solid anger.

The beast pulled on her, ripping through the shoe, but for the first time, she wasn't sure if its jagged action was out of hunger. It felt like it may have been from something else.

Her thoughts wandered through the possibilities: was it pulling back from fear?

No, that can't be.

The circle of monsters around her closed inward, and Nikka knew her questions didn't matter. There were so many. It didn't matter if that one felt something weird. They would all tear into her at any second.

The ground rumbled harder, this time from one direction, behind Nikka. She turned, and a passage opened up in the wall of insect men. It was like an invisible force was pushing them aside, and in the distance, she saw why.

It was Masha. She was standing in the doorway of her cabin. Her eyes glowed red, and her hair was on fire.

"Come!" She stared at Nikka, and Nikka felt the heat of Masha's gaze upon her.

There was a way out. A jolt shocked Nikka onto her feet, and despite the pain in her sole, she sprinted toward the tiny cabin.

She heard the wind as clawed legs swung at her, and she ran harder. She felt the earth thud as they slammed into dirt, and not a one touched her. She smelled the smoke as chitinous limbs descended toward her and flared.

She kept her eyes on Masha, on the open door.

It was ten feet away, five, one. She dove through the opening, and it slammed behind her.

"Curious." Masha kneeled and looked Nikka over. She wore a puzzled expression in her aged eyes. Nikka swore the crow's-feet had grown. Her hair was streaked with gray. Wrinkles traced her laugh lines and her neck.

She waved her hand, shooing Nikka away.

<hr>

Nikka opened her eyes in a steel-lined room with a throbbing pain in her head. Then she realized there was another in her foot.

"What?" She sat forward, and the table shook below her.

"Easy." It was Mr. Ramon. He walked over and braced her shoulder as she sat all the way up.

She was on a gurney, the same kind they had been pushing the old man on. She looked and saw the old man was naked on the steel table in the center of the room—or, part of him was. His arm was only a stump.

"Oh god." She covered her mouth and pulled away from Mr. Ramon. He took the hint and stepped back. She turned and lowered her legs over the side and saw the rest of the old man.

His legs and arms had been removed. He was nothing but a head on a torso with a dick and a pair of deflated balls hanging between two very short stumps. On the floor was an open rubber tote with sections of his limbs: his forearms, including the hands, his upper arms, his scrawny upper and lower legs. All of the man's extremities had been neatly disassembled and stacked inside that rubber container.

"I was worried about you," the mortician said. "You fainted."

Nikka trembled. She had been lying on this gurney, sleeping, as Mr. Ramon dismembered that man.

It could have been her. She knew that. If she had hit her head too hard when she fell—she had obviously hit it from the pain in her skull—there would have been nothing stopping the man from adding her pieces to that tote.

"How are you feeling?" he said.

She closed her eyes and fought to keep herself still despite the pounding in her chest, fought the urge to jump up and run. But she had to respond. She was sitting with a maniac; she had to be cool, to placate him.

"Um, a little nauseous. I'm okay, though."

"That can happen with head injuries. If it doesn't go away, you may want to get it looked at, make sure it's not a concussion."

"Yeah." She looked at her legs, contemplating the jump down. Her foot really hurt. What had she—she remembered the dream. There was no way it hurt from that bug beast. *Right?*

She braced herself and jumped to her feet. Her legs were wobbly.

"Just go slow." He turned away and put the lid on his tote. "I'll carry this one."

Gee, thanks. She didn't want to go slow. She wanted to sprint. She didn't want what she knew was coming next: that disgusting tote. It was coming with her, and she knew it. She had only brought the old man there to be processed, and he was coming with her again.

That was her next task.

Nikka sat in her driver's seat as Mr. Ramon loaded the container and shut the hatch. She didn't look inside the storeroom on her way out when she passed it. She had glued her eyes to the exit door. She didn't say another word to Ramon, only waited as he loaded.

He waved with his four-fingered hand as she drove away.

She drove toward the butcher and remarked to herself that the sun had risen while she had been out. She had seen too many sunrises while evading sleep that the idea of sleeping through it somewhat amused her. She had grown to really like sunrises, more so than sunsets. One marked the start of the battle with sleep, the other the victory.

But did it matter if she could faint and still have those dreams? She was supposed to be done with them. The potion was supposed to stop them. Was the witch lying?

"Curious," Masha had said. *What did that mean?* Masha was supposed to have the answers. She was supposed to be fixing this. How was Masha there, seemingly unsure and unable to control the beasts in Nikka's dreams?

Was this deal even worth it? Could Masha actually fix her?

It was the first time in a week that she had doubts.

Nikka really didn't want to think that way. She had had a good week. Her dreams hadn't been perfect, but she was getting through them. She wasn't dreading every night, terrified of what would come. She wasn't afraid of interacting with people for fear of her exhaustion being apparent and ruining everything.

She needed to stay positive. She couldn't let one (or two) event(s) ruin the progress she was making and the chance to end this chapter of her life and move on.

By the time Nikka pulled up at Ronald's Meats, her frazzled nerves had somewhat softened. She didn't like the tasks she was doing—more accurately, she was appalled by them—but she could find ways to justify them in her head. Whatever was happening with the totes and the mortician and the butcher was none of her business. She was just a driver, just a girl doing her job to get through this. It was only for a month, right?

She saw that old man's face as he lay dead on that pew. She saw it again on the mortician's steel table, his body with no arms or legs. It made her eyes burn.

No. He was already dead. Just get through this.

She backed up to the butcher shop's garage. She had just stopped the car when the hatch opened and Ronald lifted the tote from the rear.

He carried it inside and set it down—set the old man down.

Nikka closed her eyes and calmed her heart, calmed her breathing before she burst into tears. Then the car shook.

She saw Ronald in the mirror. He had placed a new tote in the back.

What the fuck?

She had thought she was done for the day. She wanted to grab a Lucky Shot Burger and head home to veg out and relax. That feeling (Masha) told her no. She had another task to do.

Ronald loaded another tote in the back and then a third. He shut the hatch and slapped her rear window, signifying he was done.

What the hell did he just put back there? Christ. She didn't want to know, and beyond the fact that she was at a butcher's shop and had just dropped off parts of an old man, she stopped herself from thinking any more about it.

Nikka turned up the radio. The local station played Imagine Dragons, and she hummed the melody as she hit the gas. She wasn't the biggest fan, but having heard the song a thousand times on the radio, she was sure she could hum it, especially if it meant she didn't have to think.

She didn't focus on where she was going other than stopping at lights and using her turn signals. She let Masha guide her. She hummed the next song when it came on and the song after that. She pulled into a parking lot and gasped when she realized where she was: Lucky Shot Burger.

She wondered at first if she had let her hunger do the driving instead of the witch, but her instinct told her no. It told her to go past the drive-thru line and then back up to the rear of the building between the Order Here sign and the loading door.

"No, no, no." She didn't want this to be true.

She closed her eyes, and there was a knock at her back door. Someone was at the hatch.

Fuck.

Nikka hit the unlock button, and the rear opened. She felt the car move as someone lifted a tote. A few seconds later, it happened again. And then a third time. She didn't look in the mirror or turn around. She didn't want to see who it was or even confirm if they took the containers inside or not. She wanted this to be over.

Please, let it be over.

The hatch closed and someone patted on the glass back there. Just as Ronald had.

She was free to go. She was done for the day, and she wished she had never gotten out of bed.

Nikka pulled away from the building, and by the time she reached the road, she was hungry again. The smell was coming in the window. She could taste a Lucky Shot Burger on her tongue, feel the meat rolling around inside her mouth. She wanted one. Oh, how she wanted one.

The urge was making her belly bubble. It was making her mouth water. Her heart was beating faster and her lungs gulped in air.

She couldn't stop herself.

Nikka threw the car in reverse and pulled up to the drive-thru line behind a car ordering their lunch. She wanted this. She hated this. She wanted to drive away.

The car ahead pulled up.

She stared at the menu board, still a car-length away, her mouth nearly drooling. Her hands were sweating on the steering wheel. She thought of slamming on the gas and speeding away, and her tongue was drenched in desperation.

A horn blared behind her, and Nikka jumped. She pulled up to the menu.

"Welcome to Lucky Shot Burger. How can I help you?" the menu board's speaker yelled.

All Nikka could see on the board was the ring of four-leafed clovers and horseshoes that circled the edge. She remembered the old man. Was he going to end up here in a patty? Was that what she had been eating? People?

She couldn't. The idea made her want to puke. The memory of her last bite made her hungry.

"Can I help you?" the speaker asked.

The horn behind her blared.

"One Four-Leaf Bacon Burger," she found herself saying.

It was okay. She could fight this. She didn't have to eat it. She was in the line, so she should order it, but just because she ordered it didn't mean she had to eat it. She would get the thing and take it—where? Home? To the police? They could test it and come back and do the right thing.

And she would lose everything.

That didn't matter right now. She would just get the burger. That was it. She could decide what to do with it afterward.

"That'll be six ninety-nine at the window."

"Thank—thank you," she forced out the words.

She pulled up to the window. Her skin crawled. It tingled. Her mouth watered. Her heart throbbed.

She could go to jail for this. She could rot in Hell—if she believed in such a thing. Was she really doing this?

The window opened. She reached into her wallet and handed the guy a ten. He looked at her with shiny brown eyes. There was a smile on his face.

He gave her the bag, three dollars, and a penny and shut the window.

She looked at the bag, seeing the tin-foil-lined wrapper through it. Through that she saw the meat inside. It was juicy and delicious. It was disgusting. It—

The horn again.

She dropped the bag in her passenger seat and stepped on the gas. She didn't stop until she was parked outside her apartment.

She was sweating. Her shirt and jeans were drenched.

She stared at the bag like it was her nemesis. Like it was her lover.

"No." She couldn't. But she was so hungry. It was like she hadn't eaten in weeks.

She wanted to scream.

Nikka grabbed the cup with Pastor Sander's finger. She snatched the Lucky Shot Burger bag and hurried from the car. She had to get inside. She felt it calling. She felt her seat on her couch and the TV, and that heavenly taste in her mouth.

Nikka raced up the sidewalk and turned at the entrance to the stairs. Around the corner, her foot rising to meet the first step, her brain was on autopilot to get her to her third-floor home.

Her face flashed with pain. She stumbled back as someone said, "Hey!"

She was falling. As she drifted down, she saw a red spot on a guy's elbow where her face had collided. She saw his eyes, sparkling green. She saw his shiny, brown hair. As her back hit the ground, the realization struck her that he was gorgeous.

Who was this amazing-looking man in her building, and why was she just now noticing? Was there something wrong with her?

"Are you okay?" He reached toward her. His eyes were wide and his mouth open in shock. He was like an angel.

She could have laid there all day looking up at him, she thought, but then her stomach told her otherwise. It ordered her to move.

Nikka climbed to her feet, too hungry to be as embarrassed as she should have been. All she could do was say, "Sorry!" as she raced around him and up to her apartment.

Chapter Fifteen

THE TELEVISION WAS ON, playing more old episodes of *Rosanne*, but Nikka didn't really see them. She saw the first one start with Darlene rushing to her room with a bad report card, and then the hunger got her.

The cheeseburger was down her throat before she could think of the word *No*. All that remained was a crescent-shaped edge of the bun with a small line of meat sitting in a balled-up wrapper beside the others.

She stared at them all. A little less than a dozen covered the table. They were more than just trash, more than just crumpled-up paper and bread and meat. They were a disgusting reminder of something she couldn't deny. Previously, she had been able to pretend she didn't know what was happening, but now it was right there in front of her face and there was no way around it.

Lucky Shot Burger had people in their meat. That butcher ground up human limbs for burgers. That mortician sent body parts from the dead to the butcher. That pastor sent bodies to the mortician. And she ate it.

She ate it.

More than once.

The evidence was all over her table. There was some in her fridge. There was some in her trash can.

Her whole body felt sick. From her toes to her head, she felt trembly and cold. Her insides squirmed.

That meat was in her, had been for a week. It was then, just after her first dose of Masha's potion, that the hunger hit her. And she knew she would eat it again. She hadn't wanted to eat it this time, but it happened anyway, and she knew she wouldn't be able to stop it next time either.

The potion wanted it. And she wanted—no, she *needed*—that potion. It wasn't like there was another choice. She had to stop the dreams; it was the only way.

She wanted to rationalize it, to tell herself that it wasn't that bad. The people were already dead, weren't they? It wasn't like the mortician was hunting people down and killing them. So who did it hurt?

Nikka was sure the answer was more than she wanted to know. But what else was she supposed to do? It was her life on the line if she didn't keep the dreams away.

But she didn't want to eat people. The thought made her stomach turn on end as the very meat she debated on worked its way through.

Between all the contemplation about the ethics of cannibalism, there was another image on her mind, and she could only deny it for so long: his face. His lustrous brown hair. His glorious green eyes. The image of the man in the stairwell sat on her brain, hoping to push everything else aside so she could think of nothing more.

A creeping ball of butterflies in her stomach pushed everything else to the side when she let it take hold. It was stupid. It was like a schoolgirl crush, the type of thing she never really experienced after the early days of high school and never let herself think about after the dreams started. But the dreams were passing. They would be completely gone soon. She was finally in a place where having a guy in her life could make sense.

At least the butterflies told her to think so.

Who was he, though? She had never seen him in the apartment complex before—she was sure she would have remembered that face. Maybe he was new? Maybe he was just visiting someone, but she didn't want to think that. She needed to know he was coming back at some point.

She imagined sitting at her bedroom window watching the cars come and go and hoping one of them would be him.

Nikka couldn't really do that. Was she that lovesick? Already? But the more she thought about those eyes, the way his hair jostled over his brow when he offered her his hand, it made her warm inside. It made her want to go over there and sit in the window right that minute. The pull was nearly as strong as her cravings for Lucky Shot Burger, and she wished she knew why.

He had to come back soon, right?

She didn't want to think that way. She glanced at the TV and thought she was being about as boy crazy as Becky. But then she saw the Lucky Shot Burger trash and forced herself to look away. It was better to do anything other than think about cannibalism. She would take boy crazy if she had to.

She could walk up and down the stairs a few times a day and hope she ran into him: checking the mail, walking around the complex for a little exercise, stopping by the tiny gym that she never visited and pretending she was interested in working out. She didn't know if that was better or worse than perching in her window and watching the parking lot like some obsessed sycophant.

Either way, she needed to clean the place up. If she did bump into him and just so happened to end up there, it was rather disgusting.

Nikka saw him sitting on the couch with her, Netflix and chill on the agenda. She felt herself blushing.

"That's it." She stood and started picking up her burger trash. Whatever happened next, the place was going to be clean for it.

The world was doing that dripping thing again, and Lilly hated that. It meant everything was about to go to shit if she didn't move at that instant. But she couldn't go anywhere until her target did.

She watched him step from the doors of his church and walk to a little white Honda. The way he walked actually reminded her of Pastor Sanders, and she wondered if all religious leaders shared that kind of walk. It was a kind of dainty walk, but also overly confident. Then she wondered if this guy was one of Sanders's competitors—and, did churches have competitors?

She watched his footsteps; they left traces of black slime as he moved.

He started the Honda, and she started her truck, the brown Ford Ranger that Adrian had paid fifty bucks for a month before he died. It rattled and sounded like it was dying as well, but it started, and she followed the Honda south through the west side of town.

The clouds came over Custer Falls as they drove. There was a low rumble that most people would have associated with an incoming lightning storm, but Lilly knew better. That wasn't rain; it was the witch.

The clouds were growing darker, and the Honda's shadow was black. The gloomy blob was a rolling mass, hiding in that absence of light; it was a magic form that called and guided Lilly, just as the one under Lilly's vehicle warned her forward and assured her that it would drag her to the depths of its black pit if she failed.

Drops of black goo hit her windshield. Lilly knew better than to try to clean them off with the windshield wipers as they would just smear across the glass in big oily streaks. Besides, she wasn't in danger just yet. It was more like she was on the tail end of safety. As long as she kept pace, it would be okay.

The reverend turned left, and Lilly followed. He headed south again, and so did she.

In the rearview mirror, the town was gray. A fog was moving in, covering the space between Lilly and her past. It filled the roads in the distance ahead, blocking the way to her future. She was within the confined space of *Now*, a place where every action was guided and monitored, where she was on the border of fulfilling her assignment and being cast onto the heap of devastation.

The witch had told her she had doubts that Lily could follow the path. The drugs coming out of her system was the easy step, but the addictive parts of her mind that formed the dependency, those were the dangerous bits, the deadly bits if Lilly didn't comply, the ones that would spell her suffering if she went back to her old ways. So there were timers on her jobs. There were guardrails to make sure she did what she had promised.

That day in the witch's shack, Lilly would have agreed to anything to free herself, but she hated the dripping.

The reverend parked in front of a garage at the end of a row of townhouses. They were relatively new, unassuming two-story homes with brown siding and a large driveway that stretched across all five units that shared the lot.

Lilly slowed and stopped about fifty feet away, and the man got out and performed the same little walk from his car to the front door as he had from the church to his car. It seemed pretentious now. Once he was inside, she pulled up behind his Honda and parked.

She waited as the fog moved in. She wanted him at ease when she came, at home.

Black drops patted the glass. They ran down the windshield, blocking visibility one spot at a time. She could almost see nothing when she decided it was time and killed the engine and got out.

Oily rain tapped on her head. It wet her hair and ran down her cheeks.

It stained the house as it hit the siding and ran down in thick, clumpy balls. It marked the concrete drive and sidewalk black. Lilly could feel it building up and starting to burn as she reached the door. It was bubbling up from the ground as she turned the knob. The fog was almost pushing her as she stepped inside.

She was quiet, but she was fast, her feet silent against the linoleum by the door and the carpet just beyond. She paused just long enough to listen and locate him. The man was in the kitchen to her right.

The blackness dripped from the ceiling. It was a roof of liquid oil, and a drop burned as soon as it hit her head. The carpet swelled with oil. The walls bulged with the faces of the dead as they scratched and clawed to enter her world. The birds leaned through, their inky eyes hard upon her.

She had to hurry, or they would.

Lilly turned right and stepped into the kitchen. Her shoe squeaked on the tile, and the reverend spun where he stood in front of the refrigerator. He was only shocked to see her for a second. In the next second, his eyes bulged black and his skin flashed gray. His mouth opened, and he took a step toward Lilly.

She could see the other side through his gaze. The thing in charge was frantic like someone told it that if it ate her soul, it could be free. But it was so deranged from the pain that there was no real thought there.

She stepped forward between his reaching arms and thrust her knife into his chest.

He blinked, acknowledging the pain—the real man, not the demon—and as his wounded heart attacked him, he dropped.

She watched him twitch on the tile for a few seconds, hoping he wouldn't puke. She had to deal with enough puke of her own without having to deal with one of these assholes upchucking during his death throes.

Once he was still, and the oil had faded away, she went back to her

Ranger for a tote.

Nikka finished straightening up the apartment and started the coffee maker. She wasn't necessarily tired, but the habit of downing coffee all day was hard to break, and she hoped it would help her think. There was a lot to think about, some things she would rather block out, but some she was excited to ponder.

The events of the day were on her list of thoughts to avoid, but she didn't think she should. She was involved in something, even if she didn't want to take it seriously. Yes, it was only driving and delivering, and yes, it was only temporary, but those things (dead people and parts) were in her car. She was a part of whatever was going on whether she wanted to be or not, and she needed to understand what was happening—even if only to keep herself out of trouble.

Then there was her missing roommates. How long had it been since she had seen them? Should she search their room for clues? Should she call the police and report them missing? What if they just decided to take a little vacation or something? They could have been too mad at her to tell her. She guessed that was possible.

Finally, there was *him*, the dreamboat from the stairs.

As much as she tried, she couldn't get his face out of her mind while she was cleaning. Those eyes seemed to hover in her thoughts, keeping her company as she picked up trash and wiped down the tables and counters. She had to make a plan to meet him. She just had to.

She didn't know if she had felt so compelled in her entire life. It was more than a crush; it was like her thoughts were being dragged toward him. No matter what else she tried to concentrate on, her mind kept returning to *him*.

Nikka pulled a warm mug from the recently finished dishwasher and set it beside the coffee maker. She spooned in her sugar and added her cream. The coffee maker wasn't quite finished, but it was close enough, so she pulled the pot and poured.

The dense aroma was like heaven in her nose as coffee, creamer, and sugar swirled in the rising drink. She replaced the pot and stirred, and when she set the spoon on the counter, a knock came at the door.

Nikka didn't jump. She often did when her phone rang or the door sounded. Those things always seemed to come when she wasn't expecting them. This time, however, was different. It was almost like a premonition hit her a split second before the knock came, like she knew the sound was about to happen.

She sipped her mug as she walked toward the door. A smirk grew on her face as she reached for the knob. There were butterflies rising in her stomach, but it was an odd tickle, an enjoyable one. Whatever was about to happen was exciting. Whoever it was, she was happy about it.

She knew it could be anyone: a server friend from Country Kitchen, a neighbor wanting something, the police who found Rich's and Lynn's bodies by the river. She didn't expect who it actually was.

She couldn't stop the smile from rising, practically couldn't tell it was there even with her cheeks pinned back in glee as she stood astonished by whom she saw when she opened the door.

She stared into the dreamboat's eyes, utterly speechless.

Chapter Sixteen

N IKKA WAS LOCKED IN place; it was like her mind and body were both stalled in the moment, unable to function beyond their state of rigidity.

The man standing in her doorway didn't say anything, either. He stared into Nikka's eyes as his lips curled in a reactionary grin.

She loved it. She loved the shine in his emerald eyes. She loved the way his chestnut hair flowed up and over the side of his face. She loved the creases in his skin above the corners of his smile. The sight restrained her from speaking, from saying anything at all—assuming she knew what to say.

The silence would have been uncomfortable in any other situation, with any other person, but for some reason, it wasn't. They looked at each other, almost totally at ease.

"Hi," he finally said.

"Hi," she repeated.

Another drawn-out silence.

"I'm, uh, sorry I ran into you earlier," she decided on. "I was just in a hurry, and—"

"Oh, it's okay," he interrupted.

She thought he couldn't help but look beautiful as he talked.

"I hope I didn't hurt you when you fell."

"No." She shook her head emphatically. She felt like a little kid and didn't care. He was here. He was talking to her. She didn't have to pull off any manner of stunt like the ones she had been concocting in her imagination to find him. "I'm fine. Nothing broken."

"Good."

Another pause.

Finally, something clicked inside Nikka's head. He was in the hallway, and that wasn't where she wanted him. She had spent the last two hours cleaning for just this occasion, and now she needed to make it happen.

"Would you like to come in?" She widened the door and gestured inward. "Have some coffee? I just made a pot."

"Yeah." He nodded. "I'd like that."

She stepped aside and guided him toward the couch with a wave of her hand. He was halfway there when she shut the door, and a thought formed in her mind of a spider welcoming a fly into its web.

Nikka was by no means a predator. She had almost no experience with boys, let alone men, with the exception of Bobby Hawkins in seventh grade, who asked her to the dance and was too scared to kiss her while saying goodnight at her front door. Then there was Matt French, whom she really liked at summer camp the following year, and she regrettably offered her virginity to. He failed to do more than stick his thing in once under the cool breeze and the forest's boughs before he shot his load into the condom she had insisted on.

She hated thinking about that night and still refused to count it as her first time. There hadn't been another chance for a real first time between then and that fateful day looking out her bedroom window into Sully Richardson's yard, and she hadn't looked for another once since.

She wondered if... She realized mid-thought as she started toward the kitchen that she was contemplating all of this without knowing this gorgeous man's name. She stopped at the edge of the hallway and swayed to one side, head tilted.

"I'm Nikka, by the way." She waited.

"Mark. Mark Nelson." He took a seat on the couch.

"How do you take your coffee, Mark?"

"Some creamer and sweet, like candy." He shifted in place, leaning back as if testing her for a response.

"Just like me." She smirked and darted around the corner.

In the kitchen, she felt like a heart attack was incoming. Her chest was pounding. Her lungs grasped for air. She wanted this to happen so badly, and all of her calm demeanor was evaporating. She had him in the apartment now, and she needed to play it cool. She would never forgive herself if she blew it at this point.

She pulled two clean mugs from the dishwasher and filled them. Coffee, creamer, sugar, making them exactly the same. She returned to the living room with one in each hand.

He was looking at the art on the walls, pictures of rural Montana that Rich and Lynn had taken over the last few years during their occasional trips. Nikka liked some of them, the ones of barns on the side of the road or the really small towns off the beaten path. She didn't really like the wilderness images. Those kind of gave her the creeps—or, they did now as she followed his eyes to one she was sure was a group of trees with Mount Custer behind them.

She stood there examining the image, and she realized that she didn't remember seeing that one before. It looked very much like a scene from her recent trip to Black Creek, but that wouldn't have made any sense. Rich and Lynn had never been that way—not as far as she knew, anyway.

"Is one of those for me?" Mark asked.

Nikka jerked her gaze from the photo and met his eyes. They chilled her and made her heart flutter. But what was he talking about?

He pointed. "Is one of the coffees for me?" He grinned.

She blushed as she looked down and realized she had completely lost her sense of what was happening. She had made them coffee. She was about to sit.

"Yes." She rolled her eyes and extended the mug in her left toward him. She wanted to run away at that second. If she could have vanished from existence and reappeared, hiding under her covers, she would have. Instead, she sat at the other end of the couch.

He sipped the coffee and nodded. "It's good."

She sipped her own. "Taste enough like candy?"

"Put it in a wrapper and I'll buy it." He took another drink.

She wanted to toss the mugs aside and plant her lips on top of his. She could see herself on his lap treating the next ten minutes like a scene from some Internet porn site. She had been planning on trying to find him, and here he was, like the plot from one of those, like—something hit her...

"How did you find me?" she asked. She wasn't about to admit that she would have been looking for him if he hadn't. She may have been desperate, but she wasn't going to admit it.

"I asked around what apartment was yours."

Her heart thudded. He wanted to find her. He sought her out.

"I must have made an impression by falling on my ass." She tried to sound confident, shooting for mild self-deprecation.

"You sure did." Part of his bangs fell over his forehead, and he brushed them to the side. "I just—it's going to sound dumb, but I had to meet you."

She felt warm, and it wasn't the coffee. She felt a grin creeping across her face and stopped it. She had to be cool. She had to be cool.

A few seconds passed, and he asked, "You have roommates, right?"

She thought about that, noting their absence in her mind. "Yeah, Rich and Lynn. But they're on a trip right now." She had to guess that was where they were. She didn't want to dig any deeper. "What about you?

Do you live in the complex?"

"I'm new. My brother lives on the floor below." He pointed to the right. "Below your neighbor's place."

"New? Where from?"

"Matt and me—that's my brother—we're from outside Kalispell. He got a job teaching at an elementary school in town last year. When I got laid off from my job at the fish hatchery, he asked if I wanted to come down here and look for work. It seems like a nice town."

Yeah, if you don't mind all the weird shit, she thought to herself. She obviously wasn't going to say that, though. The last thing she wanted was to scare him away.

"So, you're like *new* new. You just got here?"

"Two days ago." He sipped his drink.

"Fresh off the boat." *And he's mine.* She chuckled. She wasn't about to lose this opportunity.

"I guess so."

"I can show you around," she said. *Take you to dinner, loosen you up.*

"That'd be nice."

It was like she could see his heart thumping the way hers was. She could sense it. It wasn't like this was a sure thing—she knew she could blow it—but there was a burning inside her, a good one, that told her that he was for her. If she ignored her nervousness and fought for this, it could work. And she didn't know why, but she really wanted it to. She had gone so long trying not to even think about boys, but with her life on the verge of changing forever, she wanted this more than anything.

She asked what kinds of things he might like to see. He didn't know. She said that was fine, she would show him everything—it wasn't like the town was that big, anyway.

By the time they had finished their coffees, it was all settled and they were out the door and headed toward Nikka's car.

She hoped it didn't smell like a dead old guy or his blood.

———

It wasn't like there were any real tourist attractions in Custer Falls. There were interesting locations with morbid historical value, but Nikka didn't think those were the places to take Mark on a first date—if she wanted to consider this a date, that was. Which she did. She had him all to herself, and the vibe was there. It was electric between them, and she knew it. She just had to keep things moving.

She showed Mark the Dead King's Park, also known as the 4th Avenue Park, neglecting to mention the murders that had happened there. She showed him the Town Hall, her old employer (Country Kitchen), and Custer Memorial Hospital. She took him by the mansion district, leaving out the local legend of the murder of Zelda Kappe and her hidden fortune. She drove through downtown and pointed out the Mirror, the flashiest building in town, full of businessmen and women doing the kinds of deals she would never quite understand and leaving out that her mom once worked there and that ruined their lives.

They drove past the Huckleberry Café, and Mark pointed. "That looks like a decent place. Wanna grab a bite?"

Dinner. See, it is a date. "Yeah. But they aren't open for dinner." *And I don't want any bleach in my coffee.* "But I know some other places."

"Lead on." He nodded and gestured at the road ahead.

She didn't go where her stomach urged, Lucky Shot Burger. It wasn't just that she knew what was in those burgers, even if it wouldn't be long before her stomach overruled her brain and made her go back; it was the fact that Lucky Shot Burger wasn't the place you took a first date.

Nikka took him back into downtown. She didn't stop at the Super Star, the highly overrated steakhouse, nor did she stop at Shogun's, a decent Japanese Hibachi grill. She turned just outside downtown, right about the time she could tell Mark was starting to wonder exactly where they were going.

When she parked at a building that looked more like a turn-of-the-century Victorian home than a restaurant, he finally spoke. "What's this place?"

She smirked. "Trust me."

She turned off the car and got out. He followed her, and she took his hand in hers and guided him to the door, where a sign read Lovecraft's Kitchen.

He pointed at the sign as she pulled open the door.

"This is a restaurant?"

She held her hand out for him to pass through the opening and said nothing.

Past the foyer was a podium where an elderly man stood. He had a thin, once-black mustache and hair that was slicked back over his head, reminding Nikka of greasers from the old black-and-white movies she used to watch with Mom.

The host startled himself into alertness and asked, "Two for dinner?"

"Yes, please," Nikka answered.

His hands tremored as he sorted through the menus on his podium, gathering two together. "This way." He turned and led them into the next room, staggering yet determined in his gate.

Mark's eyes were wide as he walked with Nikka. His gaze bounced from the intricate wooden moldings to the hand-crafted ornamental plaster around the finely detailed brass sconces. He seemed to marvel at the filigreed, crimson wallpaper and the carvings in the corners of the large dining room.

"Here you go," the host said, placing the menus on a small table on the right and pulling the chair out for Nikka.

"Thank you so much." She placed an appreciative hand on his shoulder and sat. She wasn't sure if the old man had the strength to push in her chair, but she wasn't going to deny his courtesy. She lifted her rear as he pushed, and Mark seated himself.

When the host had left, Mark whispered, "Wow. I'm not sure I can afford this place."

Nikka glanced at the prices on the menu and waved a hand in the air. "It's not that bad, and I've heard it's a forgotten gem." And it hadn't had any murders that she knew about. "Besides, I'll treat."

"I couldn't." He shook his head.

"You're new in town. I insist." She lifted the menu and hid behind it, shutting off any further argument. She wasn't trying to be a pushover, and she definitely wasn't planning on buying dinner for him regularly, but she felt the need to celebrate her upcoming future with something more than a bacon cheeseburger.

"If you insist." He raised his own menu and read.

The host returned several minutes later and took their orders. He then vanished for almost thirty minutes, returning with their dinners. She had the chicken, and Mark had the fish. Each of their plates was intricately decorated with vegetables sculpted in the images of odd Lovecraftian creatures: a Cthulhu-shaped potato, asparagus bound and molded into a tentacled arthropod, peas and carrots mixed into something like a boar with two heads and a hundred eyes.

They joked about how the elderly man was the only employee in the place and how the food was both frightening and alluring. Mark talked about his love for planes and his wish to get his pilot's license, and he listened to Nikka as if she were the only person in the world. She told him about her parents and her hope of attending a regular college next semester—she didn't want to depress him, but he asked, and he took it well.

They shared stories about their childhoods, about him and his brother camping and shooting bows in their backyard, and she told him stories of trips her parents took her on to other states. They laughed at silly things like making snowmen in May when the rest of the world had summer and how every August the phrase "Winter is coming" was more common in Montana than it was to *Game of Thrones* fans.

When the host brought the check and set it on the table, Mark grabbed it before Nikka had the chance.

"Hey!" she protested. "I told you it was my treat."

He stopped mid-reach for his wallet and held up the paper that was inside the tall billfold. It had a drawing of a tiny monster, and written in cursive, it read: "$0 Thank you!"

"What's this?"

Nikka didn't know what to say.

"Do you know him or something?"

She shook her head. "Never seen him before."

"But you're a regular here, right?"

She shook her head again. "No. I've just always wanted to try it."

"Okay. Then it's got to be a joke. Let me ask him." Mark rose and checked by the front podium. With no one there, he stuck his head through the kitchen door and called.

No one answered.

He sat back at the table.

Nikka didn't want to think it, but she couldn't help but assume Masha had something to do with this. "Here." She pulled a twenty from her pocket and held it out. "Let's leave him a tip, regardless."

Mark shook his head. "Okay." He pulled another twenty from his own wallet, sealed both of their bills inside the billfold, and set it on the table. "Weird, but okay."

She took his hand in hers. They sat there for a minute just contently looking into one another's eyes.

"You ready?" she asked. She didn't really want the moment to end, but they couldn't stay there all night.

He gave her hand an extra, tiny squeeze. "Yeah."

They walked out, their hands still together.

The food in their bellies squirmed unnoticed, doing the witch's job of drawing them closer by the minute.

Chapter Seventeen

L ILLY FELT HOLLOW INSIDE as she passed the Lucky Shot Burger. It had been so long since she ate a whole meal and kept it down she had almost gotten used to the feeling of her stomach shrinking and its inner walls rubbing against each other. She had almost gotten used to the ever-present burning in her throat and the ceaseless salivating. At least the hunger had switched from drugs to food. She was grateful to the witch for that.

She didn't stop at Lucky Shot Burger because she knew she still had a bite or two in her fridge at home. That would last until tomorrow. She would eat and puke when she got there. She would go to Black Creek tomorrow for her second-to-last dose, and at least with that she would actually feel full. And then there would only be a week left.

Just one week. She could hardly believe it.

She would be done with the craving forever, a guarantee no rehab in the world could promise, and she would never look back. She would leave this cesspool of a town and it would eternally live in her rearview mirror.

But as she drove the streets of Custer Falls, her past still lived as ghosts inside her memories.

A glimpse of the 4th Avenue Park made her think of her mother pushing her on the swings and her whole family watching the Starlight Symphony at the amphitheater. She would shuffle in her seat from the bruises Mom left on her rear, but as a kid it was worth it. There was the toy store on the edge of downtown where her dad always bought her presents for a promise to keep their private playtimes a secret. There were too many ghosts in town, too many memories that would never fade, and too much pain that would continue to recycle itself in her thoughts as long as she remained there.

She parked in front of her apartment. She could smell the rot coming from inside, but she wondered if that was just because she knew it was in there. She hadn't had any complaints from the neighbors as far as she knew, though she wondered if she should take care of that ahead of time; the elderly lady to her right and the single guy across the hall could both be useful for the butcher.

Her head tilted as she mulled that over.

"After Black Creek," she told herself. She had made it this long, and she was pretty sure the witch's guiding hand had helped.

She was positive she smelled the rot when she got to the front door. It was mixed with lavender oils and plug-in air fresheners, but she could smell it. It was a month and a half worth of decay, after all. There was only so much smell the trash bags would contain.

But she was almost done, almost ready to leave town, and she would never have to worry about this again.

She opened and closed the door, slipping swiftly inside.

There were more flies. They buzzed inside the bedroom, and in the dusky slivers of light that snuck between the edges of her blinds and the window frame, she saw them. And she saw Adrian.

She smiled and blew him a kiss.

A fly walked across his milky eye and ate from the leaking liquid in its corner.

No matter what else happened, she would be ever thankful to the witch for giving her the strength she needed to kill him. Of all the baggage she had built up in her eighteen years of life, he had been the heaviest, even worse than the drugs. And he was gone.

She dropped her bag on the dried pool of blood that coated the dining room table and went to the kitchen. She took her last bite of Lucky Shot Burger from the fridge, unwrapped it, and held it over the sink in front of her.

Her hand trembled.

She looked into that burger and saw everything horrid and everything great in her past two decades of life. She saw herself snorting meth. She saw her father's wandering fingers. She saw Adrian holding her down and enjoying her screams. She saw her mother looking the other way for all those years.

She knew what was going to happen after this bite, and she shoved it all in her mouth at one time—a third of a burger—and she hoped she could at least keep down a few crumbs.

The vomit was nearly instantaneous.

Adrian heard her puking. He would have laughed if he could have moved his mouth and chest.

She was always so weak. That was why he took her. That was why he kept her. That was why she would be his again soon.

Lilly had been a junior at Custer Falls High when he first spotted her. She was walking home past the condemned Wesker Pump off Road 12, where he had been squatting with Bricks. She had that perfect kind of untarnished teen ass he loved, and as she went down the road, her backpack shifting with each sway of her hips, he just knew she was going to be his.

Adrian followed her up West Raven Street then onto Milwaukee Road. He knew this part of Custer Falls well. It was as close to ghetto as it got in that town; it only would have been worse if she had turned toward the train tracks. Instead, she went right, where only about one in five of the residents did crystal.

She checked the mail and went up the driveway.

Adrian noted the address, three houses down from one he robbed last summer and two the other direction from a senile granny he liked to drop in on and play with every now and then.

This girl was going to be a fun one. He knew it from her walk and the holes in her clothes. He knew it from the vibe—she was damaged, and he could use that.

She went in the front door, and he leaned on the tree in Granny's yard. In the distance, the chugging of the afternoon train grew louder, and he played with scenarios in his mind. He heard a noise from inside Granny's house as she flipped on her afternoon shows, and he decided her bed was a good place for an afternoon nap as he thought through his options.

After a night with Granny and a shower, Adrian waited on the old bat's doorstep. Right on time for school, pretending to be a good girl, he saw Lilly step outside.

She shut the door tenderly, careful not to alert her mom and dad, and there she went down the street. Backpack swaying. Hips moving.

Her mouth was pursed when she noticed Adrian, halfway between a kiss and tasting something sour. But when she saw his grin and he brushed back his long locks to one side, she couldn't help but smile.

He had her.

Adrian stood and walked in a slow, diagonal path to intercept her. Her eyes darted away and came back, the prey instinct looking for an exit but the damage inside bringing her back out of curiosity: Was he as damaged as she was? Was he as fun as the others? Was he going to hurt her as badly?

He knew that she knew the answers as soon as he opened his mouth. "Wanna skip school today and have some fun?"

She looked him up and down. "What kind of fun?"

He drew a joint from his pocket and placed it between his lips. "The kind you can't have at school." He flicked his lighter and took a long inhale. He knew the answer when she reached for it. He sealed the deal when they got to the Wesker Pump and she stayed to try the crystal.

He was on top of her before school let out, and she was back the next day without him asking. Just as he expected.

Lilly hated the woods. She hated coming out to Black Creek even more.

It didn't matter that she only had two visits left or that that goddamn inner voice guided her the whole way. It didn't matter that others called it the most beautiful or "the last best place." She only knew the cold winds, the uncomfortable paths below her feet, the monochrome, colorless visage ahead, and the nastiness that covered the witch's house.

The blackness dripped from every surface. The oil soaked the dirt, making mud that sloshed underfoot. It clogged up the trickle of water that tried to pass through the narrow creek. It lined the trees and the sitting log and the collapsed pile of logs that had once been the small cabin.

A magpie called from a skeletal pine behind the witch's home. A crow joined it from the other side of the creek. They both dripped blackness from their beaks. They both watched her, waiting for her to fall so they could swoop in and feast on her eyes.

It was like she could see herself through them. It was like they were her and she was hoping for a taste. She felt a lifetime of sorrow and hunger in their bellies, and she knew they were more than just birds.

As she approached, Lilly saw the old woman, cooking at the rusted stove. Her ancient white dress was in tatters, so unlike a few weeks back.

Her hair was practically pure white. Her skin was fold over fold with wrinkles, and her nails extended in long, wavy, curling things from her fingertips.

Slurp. Slurp. Lilly approached the ruins, black oil dripping from her feet.

An emaciated fox howled and ran through the dead trees behind her.

She stepped through the gaping hole where the door had been and walked toward the witch. She saw out into the world where the walls had fallen and saw only a world of death. It was as if looking through the ruins of this once-cabin let her see into another place, a hell that was shared with this forest that no human eye was supposed to see, and she only hoped that after next week, she never would again.

The stove's fire glistened in the blackness that coated every surface, from the collapsed table to the dried-up skeleton of the bed. Its flames were a curling, lively being, the only one for hundreds of yards, the only thing of color, of heat, of substance in this world drained of life.

"Lillian," the witch called.

Lilly didn't want to answer. The old hag's voice was like slimy death. She pictured the words on her skin like slugs, clinging to her ears and slithering inside her.

"Hello." She stopped halfway through the cabin. That was deep enough. That was farther inside this place of vile decay than she wanted and deeper than she would ever have if she wasn't already obligated.

The witch turned. Her eyes were beyond the pale of the dead—they were putrid and horrific. They were more like holes that helped this walking corpse to look like it had actually been human once than something of any real purpose. The fingers hanging from her necklace half swayed and half stuck to her slimy chest.

She raised the potion-filled cup, and it dripped down its edge and over her crooked fingers. The drops splashed onto the glossy black floor and were instantly drunk in, devoured.

"You're almost done," she said. Her death-scented breath moved faster than her feet, hitting Lilly and causing a sharp cramp in her guts. "How does it feel?"

Lilly faked a smile. "Good." Her voice was weak. "It feels good." She needed that potion. She could feel her mouth salivating. It was the only thing she needed. Her body was failing, wanting to fall apart from malnutrition and sleep eternally. That potion was all she could hold down. It was the only thing on the planet that could grant her life at this point.

"You've been doing so well," the witch said. "Just make sure to obey. And make sure to come back for your last dose, or the hunger... it will not be pretty."

"Yes ma'am." Lilly didn't think she had said those words more than twice in her life, the other time to a judge who offered her a second chance by not throwing her in the county jail. "I will obey."

"Good." The witch held out the potion.

Lilly took the small cup and tossed it back like a shot. The liquid was cold running down her throat, yet it coated her esophagus with the stickiness of honey, soothing the burning and the pain. It sank into her belly, and a cold wave of comfort filled her insides in a way that only drugs had in the past. It plumped her stomach and ran through her veins until she was full, and she was in heaven as tingles raced through her blood and lifted her brain into another place, a place so high she only *felt* here.

She saw everything go white, a white brighter than the sun, though pictures still formed inside her. They were pictures from her earliest years, a time before her parents treated her like a burden instead of a loved one. She saw her mother's smiling face illuminated in an ethereal glow. Then she saw her future away from Custer Falls—not in detail but isolated in elation, raised over the world with a promise of everlasting happiness.

This was the way to an eternal high she didn't know existed, and it had nothing to do with crystal or pot or anything on the Earth other than her freedom.

She was full. And she could last one more week—at least she thought she could.

Chapter Eighteen

WHEN NIKKA OPENED HER eyes and felt Mark's arm resting on her side, three thoughts registered at once.

(1) *Did I have sex with him?*

This was the first panic storm. She really liked him, and there he was in her bed. She didn't want him to think of her as a slut, that she had nights like this with every new boy she met. She knew times and perspectives were changing and that there was so much more empowerment out there about the idea, but at that moment, all she cared about was what kind of impression she was making.

She felt a loose shirt and shorts on her body as she went through the night of talking and laughing and getting to know each other, ending with a cuddle on the couch. That was right! They fell asleep on the couch, and she led him to the bed in the middle of the night to continue sleeping.

Thank god!

(2) *Please let me not get any tasks today.*

Yes, she wanted to finish her assignments for Masha and move on with her life. She wanted to do a good job and keep the witch happy to be sure the dreams would never come back. But Mark was there with her. They had had an amazing night. They were bonding in a way she thought she would never have. She needed this to continue. She wanted him in her life.

Hopefully it would be like last week and she would only have to work one out of seven days.

(3) *Are there still fingers in the fridge where Mark could see them?*

This one made her heart race.

She couldn't let him see those. No way. There was no explanation for fingers in your fridge that would make sense. A single glance at those things, and she was sure he would bolt.

What kind of person keeps human fingers in a baggy in the fridge? A psycho, that's who.

She thought hard. Had she moved them last night?

They had been laughing and drinking wine on the couch—he had gone to his brother's apartment when they got back from dinner and brought it over. He never went into her kitchen. She got them glasses of water later in the night.

It had completely slipped her mind that they were in there.

She felt herself beginning to panic. She had to hide them. It wasn't that he had any need to go into her refrigerator; he probably wouldn't, but she couldn't take the chance.

Nikka breathed deeply, embracing his smell and the sensation of his arm on her waist. If only those damned fingers weren't there, she could have just stayed there and enjoyed it.

She turned as she slid out from under his arm. She tingled as his fingers ran along her belly. She stood, and he groaned.

Nikka's heart jumped and her eyes shot wide. She watched him, and he snoozed away.

She slipped out and shut the door. After filling her cooler with ice, then fingers, then ice, she carried it into the one room she had avoided for over a week: Rich and Lynn's bedroom.

The air felt stale in there. The unmade bed, the items on the night-stand, and the wide-open closet all gave her the creeps. She felt like she was in a dead person's room. She knew that couldn't be right; they were just out... somewhere. They would be coming back one of these days; she was sure of it. But that wasn't how the room felt. It felt like everything in there would only grow more and more layered in dust, that no one would be in there again except for her to come back for her cooler or when someone packed up Rich's and Lynn's belongings.

Nikka couldn't believe that.

She went to the closet and placed the cooler on the floor, then draped one of Rich's shirts over it and studied it for a moment.

It should work as long as no one digs around too much.

She nodded and backed out of the room. She would have to find a better place for the fingers later, but the cooler would work for the moment.

Nikka went to the kitchen and started a fresh pot of coffee. Before it was done brewing, Mark was up and standing at the kitchen entrance. She couldn't help but think of that old coffee commercial where the smell gets everyone out of bed. Before she had time to mention it, he was kissing her good morning.

His lips were warm and soft against hers. She felt his bangs drift against her forehead, and his strong hands gripped her waist. She wanted to push him backward into her room and onto her bed, but she wasn't ready for that, no matter how fast her heart beat or how hot her blood ran through her body.

Not yet.

She placed her hand on the back of his head, welcoming him to the day, and they both grinned foolishly as they separated and she poured their cups.

She had nothing to cook for breakfast, so they went out. She had no tasks to do, and he was free, so they spent the day talking and laughing. By the time sunset came and a new night started, she felt like they had known each other for a lifetime.

Mark excused himself around eight. He said he had a job interview the next day, and he felt he should probably get some sleep. He left after the thousandth kiss that day.

While Nikka was sad to see him go, there was a need inside her stomach she had been neglecting since yesterday, and she was hesitant to deny it any longer. She made an order on her phone and flicked on the TV. When her Four-Leaf Bacon Burger arrived, she wolfed it down without a thought of the ingredients.

She fell asleep watching *Lost*, and she saw her parents on the beach. They told her they liked Mark.

It was dark when Nikka woke with a nagging sensation. It was the feeling that something important had been overlooked, like her rent payment was about to be processed but she hadn't deposited her paycheck, like she was driving through the wilderness with miles to go and the gas tank was on empty, like the apartment was on fire and she had no clue how to unlock the front door. It was a feeling of tightening anxiety around her chest, and it was telling her she had to move now—that was the only way to ease it.

Nikka rose from the couch, pulled toward the kitchen. The microwave read 3:01. She picked up the large knife from the block on the counter by the fridge then dressed with one hand, keeping the handle tight in her grip.

Her heart pounded. She was being drawn, and the anxiety was wrapped around her like a wire, dragging her from her room to her shoes to the door to the car.

She started the engine and drove.

Nikka had no doubt at that point it was Masha behind the pull. It was a *task* she was supposed to accomplish. But she didn't understand the urgency. She had been woken up with an urge to do Masha's tasks before, but not like this. Those were like suggestions in her subconscious; this was like a scream.

The wire pulled her down Academy, past the old mansions that had been mostly remodeled into duplexes. It parked her in front of a large rundown building—condemned by the looks of it.

The siding was gray and rotten. The tall structure looked like a termite feast just waiting to be demolished. She could imagine the insects running for cover once the wrecking ball came and the wood crashed down.

Whatever the witch wanted her to do was in there.

Nikka cut the engine and looked up and down the gloomy street. The houses were bleak, mostly unlit, and the streetlamps all seemed to be failing. A dark, gray fog was setting in, and while she was used to morning fog in the spring, this one gave her the creeps. The building in front of her told her that only bad things lived there, only sadness stood behind those walls, and there was nothing there for her but pain.

She recognized it now, or she thought she did. This was Zelda Kappe's home, the one from the stories, the murders and freak deaths in 1992. But in the darkness, she couldn't be sure. She hoped it wasn't.

Regardless of where she was, she had to go in. The wire was pulling. The anxiety only grew the longer she procrastinated.

She picked up the knife from the passenger seat and got out.

A ragged, torn letter of condemnation hung from the splintered door. Even with the warning notice, the door was ajar. There was a space between the frame and the slab that whistled as something angry cried from inside. It wasn't something she heard but something she felt. If she hadn't been a believer in ghosts before that night, she would have been then.

She sensed it watching her as she stepped toward the door. The ground was slick on the walk and the old, worn-out stairs. It was all black, and as she looked back, thinking of running away despite the pull, she saw that all the ground behind her was black as well. It was shiny, like oil. It was thick and somehow seeping from the earth as the fog came closer and darkened to an inky black.

There was no going back. There was only forward, into whatever task Masha had planned.

Nikka's hand trembled as she placed it flat on the door. She pushed, and she noticed the knife handle in her grip was damp from her sweat. She noticed the moldy smell of wood as the door widened. She heard it creak as it moved, and the sound made her spine vibrate under her skin. It was the sound of warning, the sound of a cranky voice whining, "*You should not be here.*"

She agreed. She didn't want to be there. But the fog at her back told her she had no choice. The wire, now wrapped around her heart, warned her to keep going. It was tightening, its grip pointed as if it was trimmed with barbs.

The inside was unlit, black in every direction. She pulled her phone from her pocket and, with its flashlight, lit a cone of illumination before her.

The white marble floor of what must have been a magnificent entryway at some point was coated in grime and debris, with a dark red stain directly below the balcony above. It was blood. She knew it without thinking, without wondering. It was a death scene, and only the body was missing.

As soon as that thought passed through Nikka's mind, the red turned to black. The entire floor did. It was leaking up through the surface, the same oily liquid that was coating the ground outside.

The oil was disgusting. Nikka didn't know what it was, only that

Masha must have sent it, and the sensation when it touched her shoe was one of repulsion and sadness. It showed her the dead body of an old woman lying where the bloodstain had been. It showed her the rotting flesh as it peeled from the woman's bones, waiting to be discovered. It made her look at the walls as the oily blackness dripped down their surfaces, and eyes began watching her from within. Muzzles and beaks and faces of things not quite human pressed forward, their malevolent stares outlined in onyx.

She yelped, and there was a wet, crunching sound as the rotting old woman moved. She moved like she wasn't just a vision, like she was there in that same room. Her joints creaked and her muscles slurped as she lifted herself from the floor onto all fours, and her head turned toward Nikka. Her decomposing lips hung from her mouth. She didn't seem to have eyelids anymore, but her black, slippery orbs fixed on Nikka, and Nikka screamed.

The woman pushed herself farther up. Chunks of her flesh flopped and hung from her bones, but the shiny red of her exposed, bloody skeleton glistened from inside.

The door slammed behind Nikka, and she had no other thought but to run. The direction the wire pulled was to the side, and that was where she found the stairs. She was halfway up the flight before she understood what she was doing or even thought about where she was going.

The wet, creaking sound of the dead woman's joints followed behind her. There was a sloshing noise and then another as rotting feet pressed on the steps.

Nikka reached the landing and looked back.

The woman's face had split, and the skin from the top of her head hung from her crimson skull where her ears should have been. Her mouth gaped as if to talk, but only harsh, panting noises came; and moist, hot breath swimming in the odor of rancid meat hit Nikka in the face.

She spun and felt the black slickness under her feet. It was coming from the floor there too. It was coating the ceiling and dripping, and somewhere in the distance, Nikka was sure she heard the caw of birds. Then the yip of something small, a pained fox, maybe?

It was coming from the walls, from the strange black faces suspended in oil and beyond. They mouthed as the calls came, but their voices were muted as if they were far, far away.

She ran and she screamed.

There were doors on either side of her, and she ignored them. There was a rustling sound on all sides. Something was in those rooms, and something was crawling within the walls.

Her only light bounced with her hand. It flashed on the floor, the ceiling, the walls, the door ahead. She wanted to keep it still but failed. The blackness as it moved was as shocking to her eyes as the faces and gleaming reflections from the dark, oily surfaces when the view returned.

She rushed into the room at the end of the hall and turned, slamming the door behind her. Her lungs burned as she sucked in air. Her chest heaved up and down as she pressed on the closed door, hoping it could stay shut and keep that old dead thing away.

A groan came from across the room.

It was a man, but it wasn't, and the shaky light of Nikka's phone turned an already horrible view into something that sent a freezing sensation from her neck to her fingers.

It was dressed like a homeless person in layers of dirty clothes. Its skin was grimy and marked with stains, but the skin itself was grayish white like the dead. Its face was sunken and angry, and its eyes were black and leaking the same oily nastiness that was coming from the floor and seeping from the walls.

The wetness dripped from the cracked plaster ceiling and spattered across the man's face. A drop landed between his spreading jaws as he growled and charged toward Nikka.

She watched him come, and the bird cries and the dead woman pounding on the door and the sounds of angry animals growling all filled her ears like a horrible, angry symphony. They sounded like they were all after her, like they all wanted to rip her into pieces for daring to exist there and hear them. They wanted to make her bleed and devour her just for living. They wanted to rip her into chunks and use those chunks to seed their own existences.

All of it made her want to drop her knife and her phone, to blind herself to the space and give in to the anger and nothingness... and let it consume her—just to make it all stop.

But she couldn't let that happen.

She saw the widening jaws of the monstrous man racing toward her. She saw the blackness in his eyes, the evil that was driving him, and she knew it was her or it. It was her life or its destruction. There was no other way through this, or her future—a possible future free of nightmares, with happy times with Mom and Dad, possibly even with Mark in her life—everything would be lost if she let it get any closer.

There was a clacking sound as its mouth snapped shut and opened again. A hiss as it moved faster, hands spreading and curling into claws. It stepped within a foot of Nikka, and the shaky light went black.

Her flashlight app had turned off, and her only way to see the room was gone.

Nikka screamed and ducked and thrust her knife forward. She felt grasping hands on her wrist as hot wetness ran over her fingers. Then pain. Sharp, agonizing pain. It was on her wrist—that thing was biting her.

She cried and jerked her hand back. She slashed left and right and jabbed the knife forward again and again.

Blood gushed over her. It sprayed in her mouth.

Another rush of pain, this time in her shoulder. She felt its blood hit her chest as her own ran down onto her bra and heated her breasts. She panicked and pulled away, feeling her skin rip in its mouth. She backed up on all fours, then climbed, rolled over, and crawled forward, farther into the room.

The banging got louder. The old woman wanted in.

There was a crashing noise. Had she gotten through?

The woman's moan combined with the homeless man's into a song that made Nikka shiver as she sped across the room—or was it blood loss? She could feel her essence leaking from her wounds. She wondered what would happen if she lost too much—they would rip her to shreds.

She pressed the button twice on the side of her phone, and the flashlight blinded her. The light was red, coated in her blood. She spun it around.

The man-thing, drenched in red light, was almost on top of her. He was gushing from his side. His cheek was sliced wide, and his eyeball was split in half. She had got him, but not enough.

The woman, or rather, the rotting corpse of her, was right behind him.

There was only one option. She had to kill them both.

Nikka focused on the man, visualized stabbing him in the side of the head, and aimed her light. She lunged forward, swinging, and he darted toward her, his fingers reaching for her face. She missed his face as he moved, but she adjusted. The blade sank into his back, plunging between his ribs where she prayed his heart was.

He flailed, arms swinging wildly.

The woman hissed and darted closer, surprisingly fast for a corpse.

Black oil dripped on Nikka's cheek.

She jerked the blade from his back and jutted toward the woman. The tip was about to go into her chest when Nikka's foot caught on the man's leg. She tumbled, rolled, and dropped her phone.

The red light went out as it landed screen up, but a blue, electronic glow dimly lit the room.

She shuffled back, gripping the knife, ready for the woman to come.

But the corpse was gone. It was like the woman had vanished.

Nikka spun and took in the room.

"Where is she," Nikka hissed.

The hag was nowhere to be seen.

Nikka picked up her phone. The light was white.

She scanned the space with her spotlight. The oil was gone. The sound was gone.

Back to the man.

He was dead, but he wasn't a monster, just a dead homeless man. A man she had killed.

Chapter Nineteen

I T MADE NO SENSE other than knowing the witch was involved. Nikka had killed a man. Yes, it wasn't a man at the time—at least, it hadn't looked like one. But still, she had done it, and looking down on him filled her with stinging regret. She had signed up to perform *tasks*, jobs she thought would be errands or something, but now a man was dead, dead by her hands.

It wasn't right.

Her wounds were gone, replaced by scars, but that hardly mattered as her body went numb from the realization of what she had done, and she puked beside his corpse.

She had done that. Was it worth it? Was shedding the dreams worth his life?

Nikka didn't know. All she could think of was his family, his friends, his end. He would never get to experience happiness or smile again. He would never see another sunrise. He would never get to do anything again, all because she had done that.

It was a sense of finality she had never faced. It was a thing she had done that could not be undone. She couldn't stitch him back up and fix his heart. It was something that had changed his life, changed her life, changed the world in an irrevocable way.

She was a murderer, whether willingly or not.

She wanted to crawl under her covers and cry. Whatever prize she would get from doing the witch's errands was now pointless, because she didn't deserve it. And she was sure she would soon see him in her dreams, even if she never saw another bug-man.

And yet, she felt another urge in her gut. She was being called. It wasn't like the wire that pulled her to this place; it was the feeling like all her past tasks, a subtle instruction: Nikka was to take the body to her car and drive it somewhere. Her guess was to the mortuary.

Nikka spent longer than she would have liked scouring that house. There was no running water, so she couldn't clean up well, but there were clothes turned rags that must have belonged to the dead woman, and she wiped herself dry. There was an old rug she used to wrap the homeless guy in so she could drag him down the stairs, and she heaved him into the back of her car.

It was more than she wanted to deal with, and she still needed to get the rest of the job done before the sun rose and other motorists could see her bloodstained hands and face in the daylight. She knew she had thinking to do; she had to seriously understand what she was going to do about the path she was on.

But before she could do that, she had to finish this job. Maybe she would break the deal with Masha. Maybe she would turn herself in to the police and confess to killing the guy in the back of her car. She just didn't know. She needed to get through this and get home—she needed time to process it all.

Nikka drove slowly. She wanted to speed through town, but even if she might turn herself in later, she wasn't prepared to get arrested just yet.

Slow. Calm. That was her plan for the moment.

The sun was peeking over the top of the eastern mountains as Nikka backed up to the rear entrance of Ramon and Sons Funeral home. Mr. Ramon opened the door and yawned, then he walked to the rear of the vehicle and waited for Nikka to unlock it.

Her hands trembled as they carried the rug inside. She didn't smell the putrid funk as they passed the storeroom. She didn't care about any of her senses as they moved. He tried to talk to her. She didn't hear a word of it. All she heard were noises, and all she could do was sit with her back against the wall as he unwrapped the musty old rug, revealing the prize inside.

He waved in her face.

She shook her head and finally heard what he was saying.

"There's a shower in there." He pointed. "You probably want to get cleaned up while I work."

Work. She could barely believe he would call it that. He was going to cut the man into pieces, the man she killed, and he just called it *work.*

"You don't want to go back out looking like that, do you?"

Nikka nearly burst into tears again. She was so detached from the moment that her hands rose in front of her face, seemingly lifted by some unknown force. She looked them over. They were even brighter red in the white lights of the mortuary's embalming room.

She shook her head no.

"Yeah. I didn't think so. Check the closet in there. Should be some extra pairs of scrubs you can wear out of here. They're not the most fashion-forward of clothes, but they'll get you home."

She nodded. "Thanks."

She got up and wandered toward the bathroom. *Is this how murderers support each other? Showers and scrubs, helping each other not get caught?*

The thought faded as hot water hit her skin. She scrubbed, her focus on a single-minded pursuit of removing every last drop of red. She wouldn't settle for a splotch or the pink residue that blood liked to leave behind after it dried, and this had definitely dried. She needed it all off.

All of it.

Using the small towel from the sink and then her fingernails, she worked at each speck. She coated herself in soap, but it wasn't enough. She pressed into her flesh, scraping at each dot, rubbing, scratching, fighting against layer after layer until it was gone or her own bright-red skin and blood hid the stains.

And then she sat.

On the tile floor of the shower, she leaned against the wall, knees to her chest, as the stream ran down her front and limbs. She may have been crying but she wasn't sure.

She had become a terrible person. She was worthless now. She may have been limited before with her sleep issues, but she had thought of herself as good. Trying her hardest. After today, that was gone, and she didn't know how she was going to live with that knowledge.

How could she live without thinking of this and hating herself every day for the rest of her life?

In the closet, Nikka found scrubs where Ramon said they would be. They were dark navy and made her feel like she had put on rough pajamas. She also found a trash bag in that closet that she stuffed her clothes into.

When Nikka passed back by the embalming room, the dead man was gone. A rubber tote sat on the steel table beside where he had lain, and the floor was wet.

It was as if the man had never been there.

Is that what she had done? Wiped him from the face of the Earth?

"Fuck," she whispered.

"There you are." He came from down the hall. "I was starting to get a little worried about you. Do you need help with the container?" Despite his cold attention to his work, his words were more calming than they should have been, and that made those words twist inside Nikka.

She felt a chill down her limbs, and she looked back at the tote. She had to take it. She was being urged to despite the fact it made her want to puke.

Nikka hated this. She wanted this whole thing to be over. She wanted to be back at home and for Mark to be there with her. Couldn't she just skip to that?

Get it done, she told herself. She walked to the tote and picked it up. It was her mess, anyway. She might as well see it to the end.

"Okay." Ramon led the way to the back door and held it open for her.

Nikka didn't look into the storeroom as she passed. She knew it had a new addition, and she didn't want to acknowledge that. Not now.

She drove to the butcher. She let him take the tote and load in two fresh ones.

She drove to Lucky Shot Burger and clenched the wheel tightly in her hands as the employee unloaded the totes.

She couldn't go through the drive-thru no matter how much she wanted to. She just couldn't.

She sat there with her hands balled up in fists, fighting that urge, when someone knocked on her window.

Nikka's face shot to the side, and she locked eyes with Justin. He was smiling. The bastard was smiling at her.

She rolled down the window, and he lifted a paper bag into view.

"Four-Leaf Bacon Burger, right?" He grinned. "I recognize you from the drive-thru. This one's on the house." He practically shoved it through her window.

She smelled the bacon. The grilled meat made her mouth water. She didn't want to take it. She snatched it from his hand.

He smiled and turned for the door.

She knew there was more than just a burger in the bag when she saw the bloody bandage on his hand.

She kept the bag and drove toward home.

———

Nikka would have liked to have said that she threw out the bacon burger and didn't devour it as soon as she set foot inside her apartment. That would have been a lie.

She was right about the finger. It had been in its own little fry container, next to her sandwich, and she set it with the others. She was unsuccessful at holding off her hunger for her Four-Leaf despite knowing what was in those burgers, despite what was in the bag beside it.

She hated herself afterward. She did the only thing she could think of to take her mind off of the horrors of the day, from leaving in the early morning through everything that had happened to coming back and doing the last thing she wanted to do. She lay on the couch and flipped on the television. She let herself fade into blackness, hoping Mom and Dad would be there to comfort her and make her feel better about it all.

When a knock came to the door a few hours later, she wasn't sure if she had seen Mom and Dad or if she had even fallen asleep. She spun from the couch and ran to the peephole. Her stomach fluttered as she hoped it was *him*.

She opened the door, and Mark was holding roses.

Chapter Twenty

Lilly stood outside her apartment door and watched Mark go into Nikka's. There was nothing peculiar about this, but she was struck with a measure of curiosity. She had seen Mark around the complex, especially when she was scoping out his brother for tomorrow's harvest. The fact that he was going inside Nikka's place—Rich and Lynn's place—seemed like more than a coincidence.

She noted that fact as the door closed, and she headed to her car. She would have to investigate that situation further.

Lilly could smell the fog as she got into the car. She could recognize it earlier now, sense it before she could see it, much like she could see sooner where the urges were taking her. She was turning on the car, and she already knew she was headed to the church. The pastor had another pickup for her or something.

She drove, and her stomach ached. The muscles all over her body did—

Something people rarely realize is how many muscles it takes to puke. Practically the entire body convulses in order to expel whatever sickness or poison has invaded the system. It really is a great feat of biology. But after doing it multiple times a day, every day, for almost a month, it wears on the muscles.

—She hated to think what shape her throat was in after wave after wave of acid coming up.

When she reached the church, the fog was a block away. When she opened the back door and walked inside, it was on the edge of the parking lot. The smell of smoke and suspended oil was heavy. It would be there soon.

She gripped her knife. She had known where to go, but the urge hadn't told her who the target was.

Maybe it was another patron? Lilly didn't know where Pastor Sanders kept pulling them from—she would have expected his flock to notice missing members—but he kept finding them. Yet his church was growing.

She also wondered if it might be the pastor himself. There was no way of knowing if he was still on the witch's good side or if he might have fallen off. No one was safe as far as Lilly knew. She wouldn't have been surprised to find out he had slipped from the witch's good graces.

Either way, she would know the target once she saw it.

The wood floorboards squeaked under her feet, and the pastor shouted through muffled tones from below. "Down here!"

"Great, a basement." She rolled her eyes and looked around, spotting a door that had been left ajar.

The edge of the fog came through the walls. The floor emitted drops of black, the start of the pool.

"Yeah, yeah, I'm going." She clenched her knife and pushed the door open.

Stairs led down into a dimly lit cellar. Lilly's shoes were sticky against the oily risers as she stepped down. She heard the calls of birds and moans from someone ahead.

"Oh god," the pastor said. "What's happening?"

When Lilly reached the bottom of the stairs, she frowned. She kind of hoped the pastor was her target. Instead, he stood in front of a chair where a woman was tied and gagged. She had turned into one of *them*, a possessed thing.

Her skin was grayish white, her eyes black and bleeding the same oil that was coating the floor and dripping from the wooden joists above. She grunted and jerked from the chair, trying to free herself, trying to get to Pastor Sanders.

"God can't help you with this one," she told the holy man as he backed away.

"She was normal a second ago."

"That's all it takes." Lilly walked to the woman and studied her face. She looked familiar, but Lilly couldn't place her. "One of your flock?"

The holy man didn't answer.

Of course she is.

Lilly squatted. She had never really gotten a good look at the things without them attacking her. She was curious.

The birds grew louder. There were howls coming through the basement walls, which were black and streaming. She sensed the faces emerging and a hundred eyes on her as she looked the woman over.

"Aren't you going to do something?" He backed farther away. There was a sloshing sound under his feet.

"Just a second."

The woman snapped, black flinging from her lips. Dark veins bulged from her neck.

Something told Lilly to look closer. She reached with her empty hand and lifted the woman's shirt. What she saw stunned her.

There was movement under the woman's skin. It wasn't just her muscles contracting; there was something below her flesh, and it was crawling around in there. It was like a slithering snake in some places. It was like bugs in others, lifting and stretching the skin so she could see the tiny legs moving.

Just as Lilly was about to drop the shirt and do her job, as she was thinking, *Let's get this done before they crawl out of there*, a split opened in the skin at the bottom of the woman's ribs.

It was a small hole, but it burst with enough force that black oil spurted, landing on Lilly's chin. The smell of rot made her insides clench, painful after the hours of vomiting.

A single black leg reached through the hole. There was a claw at its tip that dug into the woman and ripped her skin.

"No," Lilly whispered, but the thought was a scream.

The claw tore, expanding the hole, and Lilly could see the future if she didn't act now. Those things, whatever they were, would spill out. They would spread into her world, and even if she was lucky enough to kill the woman and stop the oil, banish the fog, it wouldn't matter. Those things would be there to stay, and they would come for her.

Lilly dropped the shirt, and her blade flew at the woman's throat. The demon jerked to the side, but the blade still caught her.

It wasn't deep. Black oil seeped out, then the face of a worm. It was covered in oil, and it hissed, revealing dark fangs.

Lilly swung again, completely missing this time.

The worm slipped through the hole and crawled down the woman's shirt.

"Fuck you!" Lilly grabbed the bitch by the hair on the top of her head, holding her tightly and feeling hairs snap and break under her grip. The head stilled, and she sliced across the throat from one side to the other. She wasn't going to miss again.

The blood that flowed was black and then red.

Lilly blinked, and the room was normal again. She slowly lifted the shirt. Only a scar remained where the clawed leg had peeked through before. The fanged worm was nowhere in sight.

"Thank you, God." The preacher slapped his hands together and closed his eyes as if he was about to testify.

Lilly rolled her eyes. It wasn't God he made a deal with to grow his congregation. She leaned forward and cut the ropes holding the corpse to the chair, arms then legs, then she turned to the preacher.

"You have a tarp or something? I figure you don't want her blood all over your holy basement while I get her ready to go."

His eyes were wide. He stared at a black worm about five inches long crawling on his bare forearm. It was the one from the demon-woman's neck. It left a black, slimy trail down his short sleeve and seemed to be spreading its small yet pointed jaws wide.

"What... What do I do?"

Lilly wasn't exactly sure. She kind of just wanted to watch and see what happened, but at the same time, she thought that might piss off the witch. She figured she should help him.

"Be still," she said. She raised the knife, pointing it at the creature. Maybe she could lift it away? Flip it to the floor and squash it?

But it was like the thing knew her plan. As she moved closer, it sped up. It raised its tiny head, and almost like a blur, its fangs were chewing into Pastor Sanders's arm.

"Shit!" He swung his arm around, trying to fling it off.

It kept biting. Kept chewing. Blood ran down his arm, and the thing's head went deeper.

"Be still!" She grabbed him by the arm.

He stopped moving, and its head was inside. She leaned closer, bringing the tip of the blade where she could stab it and pry it out, and it was halfway in—the goddamn worm had already burrowed half of its body into the man's flesh.

Lilly stabbed it in the tail and started pulling. The thing went taut. It was holding onto the inside of the pastor's arm for dear life.

He started screaming. "Get it out! Get it out!"

"I'm trying!" She pulled harder. The tail leaked black oil. The tension went tighter then loosened, and Lilly thought for a second she was making progress. Then it whipped outward against the knife, and the tail split into a forked pair of halves.

"Shit." Her eyes bulged as she watched helplessly.

It shot into his flesh like a spaghetti noodle getting sucked into a hungry man's mouth.

Chills ran through Lilly. It was inside him. There was no getting it out and no way of knowing what it would do. She shivered as she wondered what would happen and realized the same thing could have happened to her if she hadn't been fast enough in the past.

"What—What do I do?" the preacher screamed. "It's in me! It's inside me!"

Lilly stepped back and looked around the basement. She still needed a tarp.

"It's fucking inside me!" The preacher grabbed her shoulders with both hands and screamed in her face. "What do I do?"

Lilly raised the knife to his throat. "First, you calm the fuck down and let go of me." He complied, his breathing heavy and his eyes locked on her. "Now you help me do my job."

"B-b-but..."

She shook her head. "I just work here, man. You have questions? You better go ask the boss."

At one moment, Nikka was sitting with her parents on the beach. At the next, she was sitting with Mark. It wasn't odd, and when it happened, she wasn't struck with the strangeness of it. It just happened as things do in life, and she just went with it as she would have with the switch during a television show from one commercial to the next.

They each held a burger in their hands. They each smiled, and she drank in his eyes as she took another bite. She wondered how long she had until the bugs came and prayed it was a long time because she really loved this burger and she really loved him.

And then she paused mid-chew.

Had she really just thought that? Admitted it to herself? Did she really *love* him?

That wouldn't just have been a big step, it would have been a monumental one. She had never loved a boy. She had had crushes, had seen men in TV shows and on the Internet that she would fantasize about when she was alone and lonely as had happened too many times to count.

But *love*?

That was like a whole other planet of existence if it was true.

She watched those eyes. She watched him chew. She traced the curve of his shoulders and took in the shape of his jaw. Eating was one of the grossest things people could do, with mastication of food and it being squeezed down the throat by muscular contractions—the idea was actually sickening once you broke it down—but as she watched him do it, she was sure she did love him. It was gross, but she found it cute.

What else could it be, other than love, if she could watch him do that and think it was cute? She likened it to a mother watching her newborn burp and giggling, an owner of a toy dog breed watching it growl and snap and feeling like it was just their baby being itself.

She had to lean forward, her mouth as full of burger as his, and press her lips to his.

She giggled as she sat back down. She was sure her face was flushed. She grinned so big she was afraid her food was going to slip from between her lips.

Nikka hoped so hard that the bugs wouldn't come.

It was then that Mark swallowed his bite, and his face went slack. The burger fell from his hands, and the bright tropical sky went dim.

"No. Please, no," Nikka whispered. She swallowed her own bite and looked around for the oncoming brood; only there wasn't one. There was a wall of black fog moving in from all sides. The ocean crashed in waves of black, oily water, and as it soaked the beach, it infected the sand. As the sand went darker and darker, the stain moved toward them.

"No!" Nikka shouted at it. "Stop it!"

She turned back to Mark. His skin was pale gray-white, his eyes black. Tears ran from her eyes.

"Not him."

The palms behind him were soaking with black. Large, dark birds sat in the bows and watched, oil dripping from their feathers. Animals from the forest peeked through the fog as it closed in, thousands of them with shiny eyes that glistened in the darkening light. She thought she saw faces of bone and rotting meat.

Mark's ebony eyes seeped. His mouth opened, and in the oily sludge on his tongue were twitching, crawling things. They came up from his throat and slithered over his teeth.

He leaned forward on hands and knees and moved toward her. He tilted his head and came in close, came even nearer, and surprisingly, he was slow and smooth and calm. He was coming in not to attack her, but... to kiss her.

He was a monster. He was like the homeless guy in the house. He was disgusting. Yet she loved him.

She knew the plane was down the beach, hiding in the fog where it had crashed, and there had to have been some sharp metal she could use to defend herself. To kill him as he would try to do to her. But she didn't want to get it. She didn't want to leave him. She didn't want to kiss him in this state either, but as he moved in on her, she found herself unable to resist.

He thrust himself forward, pressing his lips to hers. His mouth opened and hers followed.

She felt tiny legs as things crawled from his mouth into hers. But she could not pull herself away. On the contrary, she felt herself lifting her hand and wrapping her fingers around the back of his head like she had the other morning.

Their lips were pressed together as only lovers do, and she was crying. She was helping him. She didn't know why—she wasn't willing it to happen, but it was.

She held his face tight against her own as a wave of them—slithering things, crawling things, slippery then patting on her tongue and the insides of her cheeks—moved into her mouth and down her throat. They crawled into her stomach, and she felt her insides splitting open as they moved from her digestive tract and infiltrated the rest of her body.

And she looked into his black, oily eyes, knowing that at any second he would pull away and try to tear into her the way the homeless man did, and she loved him. His skin was tightening over his frame, making him look more like a dead man than her boyfriend, and she loved him.

There was a hiss from him, as if the desiccation of his body had a voice. There was a creaking from his bones. There was a rushing sound as the monsters in their mouths hurried in a larger, faster wave.

She closed her eyes to appreciate the love he had to offer back. When she opened them again, she was in her bed, facing him, his eyes closed in sleep as hers had been.

She grinned. Tears filled her eyes.

She did love him, in the waking world just as she had in her dream.

She wanted to wake him up right there and tell him. But then she would have had to tell him her greatest fear, which she was sure would come true: she would have to kill him.

Chapter Twenty-One

NIKKA WORKED ON PANCAKES in the kitchen and smiled. The warm glow of the morning sun lit the living room curtains. Lionel Richie sang softly from the TV, playing from a love songs playlist. She flipped bacon and glanced at the door to her room.

He would be up soon.

She was floating this morning. Butterflies had her on edge, and she seemed to bounce back and forth every two minutes debating about whether she would or wouldn't tell him her revelation.

Would he say he loved her back? Would he get scared off?—it was so soon. Would he think she was a psycho? Or would he say he would be hers forever?

She had decided that her dream was just a fluke. It was a weird mashup of her old dreams and her worries. The fog, the change in Mark, the bugs, none of it meant anything, and she wasn't going to let it rule her decisions. He was not going to die, and she was not going to kill him. All of those anxieties were the worrying of a post-nightmare pessimism. She was going to finish her job with Masha, and they would live happily ever after—at least as much as people could in the real world.

She told herself those things, but there was an underlying knowledge that she was deluding herself. Below her happy thoughts, she still suspected. She still worried about what the urges and the dark clouds would push her into. Regardless, she would live in denial of those things for as long as she could.

Despite all the ifs, she knew what she felt, and she would let those feelings lift her spirits without anything to bring her down. She was making breakfast for her love—*love*, something she never imagined she would have—and she wasn't going to allow anyone or anything to ruin that.

She flipped the pancake, and the hinges of her bedroom door whined. Mark stepped out with bed head and yawned. He glanced at the stove, and then his eyes met hers—those green eyes that made her shiver every time she looked into them.

He grinned and rubbed his stomach. "Something smells good in here."

She took a step, lifted herself onto her tiptoes, and they kissed. She couldn't stop her cheeks from blushing.

He grinned. "I was talking about the food."

She pretended to smack him. "Well, it's not you. Go brush your teeth." She stuck her tongue out at him.

Mark did as he was told. When he returned, the kitchen table was set with serving plates of pancakes and bacon. Each of them had plates, utensils, and a steaming cup of sweet, creamy coffee. Nikka gestured at the table like a magician finishing a trick.

"Beautiful." He kissed her that time.

They said almost nothing as they ate. They shared glances and filled their bellies, and in some ways, it was better than talking. This comfortable quiet, knowing they were together, happy, and exactly where they wanted to be, was possibly the most rewarding experience Nikka could remember.

She didn't want it to end.

She watched him eat, and before she had a second to contradict her mind, she was watching him in her dream. She was watching him eat that burger as the fog came closer and the birds cawed. She was seeing the sand turn black and then it was him that was changing.

Nikka wanted more than anything to shake these images from her mind, but as he ate his bacon and the clock ticked slowly, second by second on the kitchen wall, she knew time was slipping away from them.

She saw his skin growing pale in that dream, and his eyes turning black. She saw the bugs, so many bugs, and she heard the tick, tick, tick as time marched ahead and they were left with only a handful of minutes together.

That dream was Masha's will. That had to have been what she saw. Masha knew what Nikka was going through, and soon she would want Nikka to take Mark like she had taken the homeless man in that house. Like it was some sick test. There was no amount of denial Nikka could force herself into that could change the future. It was going to happen, just as certainly as she knew eventually she would have to sleep again. The fog would come, and he would change, and she would have no choice.

There was only one way to stop it from happening. She was going to have to break the deal.

She didn't want to think that. She wanted to believe she could go to Masha and beg, but as strong as the urges were and the way the fog had pushed her where it wanted her to go, she knew begging wouldn't work. If Masha wanted something, Masha would get it. The witch was pulling the strings, and the way she was forcing Nikka around death and butchers and cannibals, there was no way Masha would think twice about the death of someone like Mark.

Or even Nikka.

To break the deal—to free themselves—they would have to kill Masha.

Lilly walked up the stairs to her apartment, and the smell of bacon in the air made her want to puke. She had her daily burger in her bag, ready for her to eat and then vomit up, but at least she had some hope that she would be able to keep a portion of that down. That bacon, however, it tantalized her tongue, pulling the saliva from its glands and teasing her about how good it would taste—and then she would be vomiting for an hour.

She clamped her teeth together and hurried past the offending door until she reached her own. That was when the urge came over her.

Lilly had thought she was done for the day. She hoped to go inside, take care of her needs, and get some sleep. No. The witch's draw told her otherwise.

"Fine," she huffed. She opened the door to her apartment and tossed her bag of food across the small living room onto the kitchen counter. She would have it when she was done.

She slammed the door and headed down the stairs. She let the urge guide her to the apartment one floor down and across the hall from her own.

She studied the door and the other three in that enclave. It was weird. She had only been guided to take someone from her own building once before—Rich and Lynn—and that was weird too. It made her more nervous about getting caught than usual. *You don't shit where you eat.*

But the urge was always right. She hadn't gotten caught yet.

She tried the knob, and it turned. She opened the door.

A smell caught Nikka's attention, making her stomach turn uneasy. It crept past the scent of bacon that filled the kitchen and snapped her from her thoughts and into reality. It was the odor she had faced in that abandoned house. It was the odor that filled the space when she was being chased by that fog.

It was her nightmare coming to life. The fog was going to surround them, and it was going to make her kill Mark. She knew it was happening—she paused as she began opening her mouth to tell him to run—but she wasn't feeling an urge from Masha.

Why was she smelling the fog if Masha wasn't calling her to kill him (yet)?

"Do you smell that?" Mark asked. He was looking around the room. "What is that?"

At any other time, him acting like that could have given her a panic attack; the last thing she wanted was a bad smell in the apartment with him there. He would think she was dirty and her place was gross. It could have driven him away. But the fact that he smelled the fog too meant she wasn't imagining it. It meant something else was going on.

"I smell it." She stood and went to the window. There it was. The black gloom was filling the parking lot and closing in on the building. But if it didn't want her, what did it want?

She felt Mark behind her at the window. His chest was against her back. She loved that feeling. It made her legs tremble, and it made her want to stand there forever despite the fact that something malevolent was coming.

"What is that?" he asked.

"Something bad." She hated to do it; she slipped away from him toward the door. "We need a better view."

He followed behind as they left their plates and coffees on the table, walking outside in little more than pajamas—though Nikka grabbed a knife from the counter as they passed.

From the common area between Nikka's front door and the three others that shared the space, she could see to the south and to the north. The view didn't provide any relief, only confirmation that the fog was coming from both sides. It was closing in on them, and she tensed as she worried what would happen next.

There was a whine from a door and then a slam from the north side of the stairs.

"Charlie?" Mark called. He started toward the north stairwell. "That you, Charlie?"

"What is it?" Nikka followed.

"That sounded like my brother's door."

Nikka wasn't sure how he could discern one door slam from another, but it was worth checking out if he was worried about his brother.

"Ugh." Mark covered his nose as he passed the last set of doors before the stairs.

There was an ungodly stench, a moist, rank odor of rot, and Nikka covered her face. It was as bad as the hallway in the mortuary, and if it was coming from a neighboring apartment, she wondered how she missed that smell before.

They didn't slow down to investigate. The fog was closer, almost touching the edge of the building, and they descended the stairs, black stairs slick with oil. Around the mid-flight landing. Down onto the second floor.

Their feet were sticky with the muck. It covered the cement pad between the second-floor apartments. It was seeping from the walls. The sconces outside each apartment entrance dripped.

Mark grabbed the knob and turned. "Charlie!"

Nikka had to look around him. Much of her view was blocked, but in the living room, she could see a woman. She could see a man on the couch, gray-white skin, black eyes, mouth open.

"Get away from him!" Mark rushed toward the woman.

The woman spun at the sound of Mark's voice. She had a knife in her hand, and Nikka immediately recognized her. It was Lilly, from her dream, from school so many years ago. But why was she there?

Lilly raised the knife, and Mark halted in his tracks with three feet between them.

Charlie rose from the couch.

"Stay back!" Lilly swiped with the knife, cutting the air.

"Get out of our house!" Mark yelled.

Lilly's eyes went from Mark to his brother and back to Mark. "He's gotta go down." She shook her head and stepped to her right.

Nikka moved closer.

Black dripped from the ceiling. Howls came through the darkening walls.

"Charlie?" Mark moved toward his brother. "Are you okay?"

Charlie hissed as he closed the gap, his hands reaching out toward his brother.

"Mark, stay back!" Nikka reached to grab Mark's shoulder. Fear shot through her as she remembered that house, the way that monster went after her. Charlie was likely just as bad. "He's dangerous!"

Mark's gaze went to each of the three others in the room. As Charlie's hands seized Mark's biceps, his jaws widened, and Mark grabbed Charlie's throat and screamed, "What the fuck?"

Charlie pulled and jerked. His mouth snapped as he tried to bite Mark's face.

"Told ya!" Lilly pointed with her knife. "You gotta kill him." Her eyes went to Nikka, and there was a brief flinch before she turned back to the brothers.

She recognized Nikka, Nikka was sure of it.

"Charlie! Knock it off!" Mark screamed.

Charlie released his brother's arm and punched him in the face.

"Charlie!"

Charlie did it again.

Mark's face glowed red. A stream of blood ran from his nose.

"We have to kill it!" Lilly shouted. She took a step toward Mark and Charlie, and Nikka jumped between them.

Charlie wound back to punch his brother again, and Mark grabbed the arm while leaning in and hooking his ankle behind Charlie's leg. Mark pushed, and they both sank to the floor. There was a thud as the brothers landed, Charlie's back slamming the thin carpet.

"We have to kill it!" Lilly screamed at Nikka.

"Stay back!" Nikka yelled.

"There's things inside him!"

Nikka was puzzled by that, but she didn't have time to think about it. Lilly charged, her knife rising. Nikka grabbed Lilly and spun her around then shoved her, and Lilly smashed into the wall face first, coming away with black oil dripping from her cheeks.

"Fucking bitch!" Lilly pointed the knife at Nikka and charged again.

Mark lay on top of his brother, holding him to the floor and narrowly evading snapping teeth. Charlie screamed with a noise that sounded more beast than man, and black oil ran from his eyes.

Nikka dodged Lilly's knife and punched the other woman in the face. Lilly swung her blade, and it sliced into Nikka's shirt as Nikka jumped back. Nikka punched again then raised her knife, and Lilly lunged at her. They grabbed each other's wrists, and Lilly's back hit the TV stand. She spun, and with Nikka holding on, they both hit the ground.

Black ooze coated Lilly's back as Nikka lay on top of her. Lilly's knife slipped from her hand, and she grabbed Nikka's blade hand with both of hers. Nikka jerked and rocked and pressed her blade toward Lilly's face.

Nikka couldn't help but hear the howls from beyond the walls. She looked into Lilly's eyes as they struggled over the knife, and from her periphery, she sensed the glares from behind those walls. She and Lilly were being watched. They were a spectacle for whatever monsters lived inside the fog and the oil, and she dreaded what would happen if she was actually confronted with whatever hid behind the blackness.

She glanced up and saw the strangely shaped faces bulging through. Angular and hungry, humanlike and beast, they stared, coated in oil, pressing closer from the other side.

The brow ridges, the eye sockets, all were close to human but eerily in the wrong places. The mouths misshapen and pulsing, hoping to eat. The broken bent and missing noses. They were a gallery of wickedness, pain, and monstrosity.

"What is that?" Mark screamed.

Nikka had to look.

A clawed finger was reaching from within Charlie's mouth. It was black and long, but rather than stiff like a finger should be, it was flexible, more muscle than bone. And then there was another. And another.

"You have to kill it," Lilly hissed. "This won't stop until it's dead."

Nikka knew she was right. She remembered the world shifting back to normal in that house once she had killed the homeless man.

Mark's brother had to die.

"Kill him, Mark," Nikka shouted. "You have to."

Another finger reached from inside Charlie's lips, and together, the fingers spread Charlie's jaws apart and shoved back the flesh of his face. They were stretching his mouth, holding it wider as if they were making room for something, something way too big to be inside a person.

"Kill Charlie?" Mark glared at her. "He's my brother!"

Charlie's mouth began to rip at the corners. His eyes bulged within their sockets. His eyeballs lifted and spread from their holes, and a sea of black poured from every orifice.

Mark screamed. Tears ran down his face. "Charlie!"

As both eyes hung on opposite sides of his face, black worms crawled from the sockets. A pair of eyes appeared in the back of Charlie's mouth, and his facial rips widened toward the back of his jaw.

"No!" Mark screamed and jumped off his brother. He stumbled as he backed away, unsure what that thing even was.

Charlie lifted his head, and worms scattered to the ground.

"Kill it," Lilly shouted at Nikka.

Nikka had to do it. Mark had fallen apart. He was in the hall, wringing his hands, looking up and down at the madness in his living room. She was the only one who still had a weapon.

She thrust herself up and off of Lilly. She raced on hands and knees across the room, black muck clinging to her knuckles and dripping from her fingers. She lifted the knife high.

"No!" Mark yelled. He turned away.

As the blade came down, Nikka saw the jaw crack downward and the face pushing through. It had deep-onyx reptilian scales. Its eyes were red. There were fangs, an underbite that pressed into the hard ridges of its upper lip.

She closed her eyes as her steel plunged into Charlie's chest. There was a brief second where she felt his heartbeat rise through the blade and thump against her hand. And then it stopped.

The room flickered, and a blink later, the walls were white and the howling was gone. Lilly was stomping on the floor, smashing black worms under her shoes. Charlie's countenance was his own, other than a jaw that barely clung to his skull.

Mark covered his face and wept. He didn't see the black worm climbing up his leg.

Adrian blinked. His fingers curled. They creaked under his dead, drying skin. That didn't matter, nor did his blurry sight. It would be enough to kill Lilly.

Chapter Twenty-Two

NIKKA PULLED THE KNIFE from Charlie's chest. She kept her eyes on Lilly, and she backed away toward Mark.

"He's dead," Mark said. "You killed him."

Lilly picked up her knife and sat in the chair beside the couch. She watched.

"You saw him," Nikka said. "He was trying to kill you."

"That…" He looked around the room. "That couldn't have been real. We were hallucinating or something."

"It was the witch," Lilly said. Her head was cocked as she tried to put it all together. "You guys are connected to her, aren't you?"

"The Black Creek Witch," Nikka muttered.

"Yeah."

"We're crazy." Mark shook his head. "We're all crazy. What do you mean *witch*? Witches aren't real."

Lilly smirked. "If you don't think what just happened was real, you're the crazy one."

"She took away my nightmares," Nikka said.

"Yeah." Lilly looked away. "She took something from me too."

"You're both crazy." Mark pulled away from Nikka. He glanced at his brother and had to look away. He backed down the hall toward the front door. "I need my phone. I need to call the police. You two killed my brother."

"Mark, no." A cramp tightened around Nikka's chest. This couldn't be. She had to kill Charlie. She didn't have a choice. He would have killed any of them, including Mark, if they had given him the chance. Now Mark blamed her. He was going to walk out of her life—the man she loved, now that she had finally discovered what love was—and he wasn't going to forgive her. There had to be something she could do, some way to fix it.

Her hands trembled with fear, real fear, maybe worse than in any of those nightmares she had been running from.

"My phone's upstairs. I'm going to get it, and I'm going to call." He grabbed the door and pulled it open.

Nikka took a step toward him, raising her hand, reaching out.

Mark stood there silently for a moment. It gave Nikka a flash of hope—maybe he was having second thoughts? Then she saw the shape of another person in the doorway beyond him.

Something moved between them. Nikka couldn't tell what it was, but Mark shifted and slowly pivoted toward the inside of the apartment. Her mouth fell open, and her stomach dropped as he walked back into the room.

He held his chest where he gripped what looked like a small stick. After a moment of Nikka's brain calculating the impossible, she recognized what it was: the handle of a knife.

A knife!

There was a knife in his chest... and his blood was spreading ever outward from that spot. Soaking into his shirt. Staining it red.

Mark opened his mouth to speak, but a gasp came out as he dropped to his knees. The look on his face was somewhere between desperation as he clutched the knife's handle and sorrow as his eyes rested on his brother.

He fell forward on his face, and Nikka took a step toward him and then stopped. She saw what was in the doorway.

At first, she thought the fog was back, that the black oil was returning, because what stood in that doorway was not something from the regular world. It had the same grayish skin, the same look of death though its eyes weren't black. They were milky white and rotten.

"Adrian!" Lilly screamed.

She knew him?

He stepped over Mark's body and continued into the room.

Nikka could barely watch. She couldn't believe what she was seeing. Blood soaked the carpet, stretching from below Mark across the plush, beige fabric that covered the floor. She felt her heart ache inside her chest. It was like it was being torn in two, and there was nothing she could do other than watch as her love's murderer strutted closer.

"He's dead," Lilly mumbled to herself. "I killed you!"

He stank. Nikka wanted to cover her face from the stench, the odor was so atrocious. It was like she could taste the foulness in the air.

"And now I'm back." Adrian spoke in a cracked gravelly tone. He paused and reached down. He turned Mark onto his side and gripped the knife. There was a wet ripping sound as he yanked it from Mark's chest. "You didn't think you could get rid of me that easily."

He walked toward Lilly. He was almost within Nikka's reach, and she hurried backward to get away from him. Her back touched the wall, and she froze against it.

"Why?" It seemed to be all Lilly could get out. By her shakiness, Nikka thought she knew all she needed. This thing had meant something to Lilly; it had also meant terrifying pain.

A crackling smile spread over Adrian's lips. "I guess you failed to keep your end of the deal, because the witch sent me to clean up your mess." He waved the knife at her. "I'll make it quick. Well, kind of."

He walked steadily toward Lilly. There was a wet squishing sound with each step. He reached with one hand toward her throat, and she launched from her seat and jabbed her knife into the left side of his neck.

It didn't stop him. He didn't even bleed. He seized her below the chin and lifted her from the floor.

Lilly gagged, and he raised her higher. Her face turned red and then darker. Her eyes bulged. Gurgling sounds came from her mouth, and the dead-man's smile widened.

"I would just end you like this," he said. "I like seeing you like this—that look in your eyes when I choke you always turns me on. But the witch, she wants your blood to spill." He held the knife up where she could see it clearly. "She wants—ck... ck... ck..." He stopped speaking with words, and something more like a clicking noise was all that came out as Nikka drove her knife into the right side of his throat and started sawing at his flesh.

Adrian's hand loosened, and Lilly dropped. She breathed in a raspy breath and snatched the knife from Adrian's hand and planted it inside one of his disgusting eyes.

He fell to his knees, and Nikka held tight to his head as she continued sawing into his neck. Putrid liquids leaked from his face as Lilly pulled out the blade and jabbed it into the other eye.

Gagging noises and slurping sounds came from his open throat. When his head was held on with nothing but a small patch of rot, Nikka let go.

Adrian thudded on the floor. He twitched, his body trying to understand what had happened to its head. When it stilled, the entire room seemed lighter, the walls farther apart.

Nikka studied her hands. They were covered in slime or something, something rotten that had leeched onto her from his skin. She glanced at Lilly, then turned to Mark.

He was still lying where he had fallen. He was indeed dead—she hadn't seen it wrong.

Nikka walked to Mark and dropped to her knees. She leaned over him and looked into his beautiful yet vacant eyes, and she cried. She saw her hopes of them having a future together drain from his chest into the carpet in diminishing waves of wet crimson. The possibilities of living together, of sex, of marriage, of kids, of experiencing life and growing older were all gone. The entire relationship had been a whirlwind, and she knew it had only been a few days, but those days felt like so much longer. His loss, more than anything she had witnessed or been a part of over the past few weeks, felt like a crime. A *real* crime. And someone needed to pay for it.

They sat like that for a while, Nikka crying and Lilly catching her breath as her throat relaxed. After a few minutes, there was a calmness there, even with three dead bodies in the room.

It was like Nikka and Lilly came to the same thought at the same time, the conclusion that was inevitable from the beginning as far as they saw it.

"We have to kill her," Nikka said. The witch had caused Mark's death, encouraged people to become cannibals, and made her kill that homeless man. And Nikka was sure that Masha would be coming for her if she didn't continue to comply, either with her monstrosities or within her dreams. Her dreams had been bad before, but they hadn't actually killed her. With the scars on her foot and hand, though, she wasn't sure that would be the case from here on out.

"We have to kill her," Lilly agreed. The witch had sent Adrian, the only one that had hurt her more in her entire life than her own parents. It was only a matter of time before the witch sent someone else. It had been hell getting off the drugs, but she was sure she could do it herself if she had to again. "Fuck that witch."

They said little more as they got up and walked out.

They were barely out of the apartment when Mark's body twitched and he started climbing to his feet.

Nikka raced through her apartment, getting dressed and grabbing a few things she thought they might need and stuffing them into her backpack. She stepped into Rich and Lynn's room and had to pause for a minute as she took in the sights and smells of what had been theirs, and it rocked her insides as she processed the fact that her roommates were dead.

She hadn't really thought about it, not clearly, anyway. As she looked over Rich's knickknacks—a small photo of his mother, a third-place trophy for a mud triathlon held every year by drunken college kids, a stack of beads he and Lynn brought home from their trip to Mardi Gras a few years back—Nikka's heart fluttered inside her chest.

She had no proof, but they hadn't been home in weeks. Wherever they were, they were surely dead, and she had done nothing to find them or even think of them. She assumed it was part of the haze the witch had her under: do the tasks, eat the burgers, come back for more potions. But she should have done better. She should have remembered them.

Her tears came back.

She remembered Rich's kindness, how he always had a calm and easy way about him, how he always asked how she was without judgment. She had never gotten along well with Lynn, but she could tell Lynn wasn't a bad person—it was just the circumstances. Lynn was worried about Rich, and though her expressions came out sour, it wasn't something Nikka could fault her for.

Nikka had to do something when she came back, something to let people know and something to try to make it right that she neglected them. But for the moment, she had to borrow something.

She walked around the bed to the far side of the room and sat by Rich's nightstand. She knew what was in there, though she and Rich had only spoken about it once.

He had been looking out for her, warning her that if anything ever happened when he wasn't there she could go to his nightstand to protect herself. She remembered the serious expression on his face, the kindness and concern.

Nikka pulled open the drawer and slid a magazine aside. There it was, shining at her, Rich's silver revolver.

She didn't want to touch it. She knew it wasn't going to go off just by touching it, but there was power in that thing, and she wasn't sure she could wield it safely.

But did she have a choice?

She took a breath and picked it up. She felt the weight. It was heavy. She imagined pointing it at Masha, and cold fear ran through her veins. What if she screwed up? What if the witch had some kind of defense?

It didn't matter. She was on the path now.

She slid it into the front pocket of her backpack and zipped it up.

When Nikka went back to the living room, Lilly was standing by the door with a backpack of her own.

"Ready to kill a witch?" Lilly asked.

Nikka understood it didn't matter if she was ready or not. It had to be done. "Let's do it."

They drove toward Custer Falls National Forest, and Mark stepped into the parking lot, following them.

Chapter Twenty-Three

EVERYTHING NIKKA SAW UPON their arrival told her the forest was not happy to see them.

Though it was barely noon when she stopped her vehicle at the Laurel Trailhead, the gathering of overcast clouds made the day feel much later. The wind had risen, dropping the springtime temperature from what had been a warm morning to somewhere in the low fifties. Together, what she saw added up to a cold and dark forest that swayed as boughs moved and creaked and groaned like something old, something angry, something that warned them away with bitterness and consternation in its temperament.

None of that dissuaded Nikka. She had enough fury stoked inside herself to provide warmth and energy. The ride from the apartments with Lilly compounded her sorrow at Mark's loss like pressure and heat forming coal, and she was ready to let it burn.

Nikka's previous illusions about Masha had completely dissolved. She had thought the woman was her friend. She had thought they had a bond and were simply helping each other to achieve their goals. The more the events of the past few weeks circled in her mind as she drove, though, the closer she came to what she was sure was the truth: she was being used like a puppet.

There was evil thriving in Custer Falls. She wasn't sure of the extent or the purpose, but it was there, and she had been helping it grow. The death at the church, the dismemberment at the mortuary, the grinding of humans into meat at the butcher, feeding it to unknowing customers at Lucky Shot Burger, it was all a scheme to spread that evil and corruption. And Nikka had been used with the simple payment of a cup of herbs and some mystical words.

But did it even work? Or was it all some placebo, mental manipulation to make her think she was being helped while all she needed was to take control of her dreams herself? Yes, she had tried a thousand things before, and she was truly on the verge of ending her curse, but had she known what she would be doing—the evil she would be causing—she knew she wouldn't have agreed.

She had known there would be a cost—*there's no such thing as a free lunch*—but this... She couldn't help but remember Mark, the blood, him lying dead on that floor... This had been too much. He was what she didn't know she needed while showing her what was out there if she looked. He was a love she didn't know she could have.

Masha taking Mark from her—that had turned into a blazing fire inside her stomach, a storm that demanded retribution, one that promised that the return of her nightmares was worth Masha's death. Even if it drove Nikka to her own grave, she would take Masha with her.

They walked toward the woods, and Lilly shined with a slick layer of sweat over her face, even in the chilling wind. Her hands twitched so much that Nikka could see it through her jacket. It was like she was going through some kind of withdrawal and it was only hitting her harder as time passed.

"You ready for this?" Nikka asked.

Lilly patted the knife on her belt. "No turning back now."

"Okay. You just—you don't look so good."

"I don't feel so good either. It's like she's sucking out all the strength she's given me, and all I can think is killing her's the only fix."

"What if it isn't?"

Lilly chuckled. "Well, at least she'll be dead."

Walking onto the trail was like stepping from dusk into night. There were shadows over shadows, and seeing farther than a few dozen feet into the forest was difficult.

Nikka felt the woods shift around them as they walked. The trees seemed untethered to the earth. The way the branches hung threatened her, warned her that she was a small thing, insignificant to the greater organism that was the forest.

And she felt it watching them. She felt it measuring them.

"I hate this fucking forest," Lilly said as if reading Nikka's mind.

"Yeah." Nikka imagined the eyes in the shadows and in the branches above. "I used to think it was pretty."

"Not anymore."

"Not anymore."

They walked in silence for a while, each watching the woods on their side, both watching ahead and repeatedly checking behind. Nikka remembered her stay in the tent, the terror that night. She hoped they would get to Black Creek before nightfall. She had the gun, of course, and between that and her anger, she felt pretty good about killing any wildlife that showed itself. But she was still afraid. The night in the woods was a supernatural place—she felt it before and felt it now—and she was concerned that the gun wasn't going to be enough.

"What did you ask for?" Lilly said. "I told you mine. It couldn't have just been dreams like you said back in that apartment. What did you really need help with?"

"Nightmares," Nikka said.

A twig snapped underfoot, and the wind howled through the boughs. The forest was talking, telling her it had plans.

She tuned it out. She had to.

"Nightmares?" Lilly shook her head as if that was the silliest thing she had ever heard. "Really?"

"I guess more like night *terrors*. They were so bad I probably didn't sleep for more than an hour or two a night. I was hallucinating—having dreams while I was still awake. I was close to killing myself it was so bad."

"Shit," Lilly muttered.

"Yeah."

"And she stopped them? Well, sure she did. You were doing her *tasks*, right?"

"Mostly. Enough so I could sleep, at least."

"So we have to do this today. Before you sleep again." Lilly wiped the sweat off her forehead and shivered.

"I don't know how she could make my dreams worse than they were, but I don't want to give her the chance."

"At least she didn't bring your ex back from the dead to kill you. I was close to finishing our deal."

Nikka shuddered. She had no ex, but the image of Adrian walking into Charlie's apartment practically dripping with death was horrifying. What he had done to Mark...

"I hated that fucker. He's the one—" Lilly rolled her eyes and sighed. "I can't blame it all on him. I wanted the drugs too. But I can blame him for every time he raped me. He needed to be dead. And if that witch sent him after me, there's no limit to what she'll do."

There was a sense between them that neither had any other options remaining. Nikka definitely didn't like this girl—she knew Lilly had been under the witch's command, but there was blame there that couldn't be avoided. Blame for Charlie and Mark, and she couldn't shake the sensation there was more going unsaid between them, that Lilly was hiding more than she was sharing. That was okay for the moment, until they had finished this last *task*, at least.

They came to the fork in the path and turned toward Rocky Bottom. They didn't have to speak about it. They both knew the way, and that made the trip feel both more comfortable and more frightening, reinforcing the fact that this was really happening, that they were doing this, and that the witch had more customers than just either of them.

They were about halfway to Rocky Bottom when the knocking of branches and the whipping of the wind were joined with other sounds in the wooded shadows. Twigs snapping. Footfalls and sliding feet over the forest floor's debris.

Something else was out there with them.

Nikka tried to ignore it for the first few minutes. There was so much noise from the wind already she was hopeful it was just more of that, hopeful that they would pass it and the noises would cease on their own.

It didn't happen.

"You hear that?" Lilly whispered. She held up a hand and stopped. "What is that?"

Nikka stopped, but she didn't want to. Of course she heard it, and more than stopping to listen, she wanted to run.

"We need to keep moving," Nikka said. "There are animals out here."

"I don't think that's an animal."

Maybe it was, and maybe it wasn't. Nikka wasn't going to stand around and wait for whatever it was to jump out onto the trail. She tugged at Lilly's arm. "Come on."

They both got moving again. Faster.

The wailing winds seemed louder as they hurried. The rushing onslaught of air whipped across their faces, and cracking and crashing noises, the noises of breaking boughs and colliding wood, masked the stomping feet that Nikka knew was just behind the closest row of trees.

There was a repeated boom, a thunderous sound as if something weighing a thousand pounds was racing through the woods. Tracking them. Waiting for its chance to attack.

It was closer. It was just beyond the shadows, and Nikka had to do something.

They ran side by side, and Nikka slid her backpack around to her front. She pulled the revolver from its pocket and gripped it in her hand.

Lilly took out her knife.

"What the fuck's out there?" Lilly screamed.

"It's not a wolf!" Nikka screamed back. "I don't know!" She suspected what it was, but she wasn't going to say. What she imagined, what she feared, couldn't have been real. The noise, the thundering footsteps, the size all seemed to match, but those were just dreams

But they weren't just dreams; she knew that. She saw them in Sully's backyard. She saw them with her own eyes. They were what caused the dreams, no matter what the head shrinkers tried to tell her, no matter how many people told her she was suffering from a hallucination or PTSD or any of that garbage.

There were monsters in the world, real ones. And it sure as hell sounded like one was right on the other side of those shadows.

"You have a gun?" Lilly shouted. "Shoot it!"

Nikka wanted to. She wanted to take out all the backed-up rage and fear that had been building in her system and unleash all six bullets. But she had to be able to see what she was shooting at.

"I will," Nikka answered.

The trail turned ahead. It was a detail that Nikka remembered. There would be a small clearing, and after a little bit, they would reach the turn to Rocky Bottom.

Good, she told herself. "Keep running! I have a plan!"

They turned with the path. Nikka was sweating under her layers. She imagined how it was going to go down, planned her actions, planned on taking those things down, whatever they were.

Nikka and Lilly reached the clearing, and Nikka stopped in its center. She planted her feet and held the gun in both hands, swinging it back and forth toward one side of the trail and then the other. One set of footfalls and then the other.

"Get behind me!" she told Lilly.

Lilly's eyes were wide, and her face was red. Her chest heaved, and her expression was one of raw fear. She did as she was told, standing behind Nikka, leaning away as if to shield herself from whatever was coming.

The wind was stronger in the clearing. It was like the cold sky was swooping down from above the canopy and blasting them in the face. It carried a scent Nikka knew was from the witch—she knew they were coming. It was a mix of burning sulfur and charred sage. It corrupted the forest's pine smell and emphasized to Nikka what she already knew: whatever was coming was sent by Masha. Maybe it was to punish them, and maybe it was to tie up loose ends—Nikka wasn't sure which or if it was both—but whatever was coming was sent by her.

The ground vibrated, making Nikka feel like she was floating. It was boom after boom in a successive rhythm. Left then right, no gaps between thumps, no waiting or pausing or searching for direction. Those things knew where they were going, and they crashed through trees and moved relentlessly toward Nikka and Lilly.

A pine on the left side of the trail collapsed with a deafening crack. Another crashed from the right. Shapes formed in the gloom, large shapes, twice the size of normal men.

The gun shook in Nikka's hand as she moved from left to right, centering her aim in the shadows where the beasts were.

"Shoot!" Lilly screamed.

But Nikka couldn't, not yet. She needed to be sure. She had to know what it was, to know for sure it was real and not a misty delusion Masha was putting before them to scare them off or waste her bullets.

"Hold on!" Nikka told her. "I need a shot!"

The shadows solidified, but not in the shapes Nikka expected. She thought she would see the bug-men, the things that rampaged in Sully's yard and haunted her dreams ever since. These were in some ways more monstrous.

They vaguely held the shapes of men, but they were not human.

Multiple large arms the size of tree trunks swayed from their shoulders. But they weren't quite arms—they didn't have hands, more like thick slugs with clawed ends. Their bodies were bulky and matted with fur, and their heads reminded Nikka of snake skulls, only a dozen eyes lined their heads from their mouths up to their cheeks, where slits opened and closed on the sides of their faces, exposing extra sets of jaws.

They were beasts made to grip and break and tear their food to shreds. And their dozens of eyes were fixed on Nikka and Lilly.

Even more bizarre than the look of the disgusting monsters that Masha had summoned was a strange sensation that Nikka felt in her bones, a thing she knew was true no matter how terrifying their appearances were or how much her eyes insisted that what they beheld was true. Nikka saw something familiar in these beasts, something hiding below their muscles and deformed bones, something she knew well and held close to herself.

"Shoot!' Lilly screamed as they moved closer.

Nikka wanted to stop them, but she was conflicted. That feeling in her gut—what if it was right? What if there was more to these monsters than the witch's evil? Or what if that was Masha's plan—to confuse her and make it easier for the beasts to rip them to shreds?

Nikka couldn't take the chance. She had to shoot. But looking at these abominations made her wonder where. Their chests were a big enough target, but would the bullets from her gun make it through that thick, matted hide? The head was huge, but what if the skull was too dense?

Nikka always heard you couldn't kill a bear with a handgun because its skull was so thick—Rich's gun wasn't that big.

She had to do something.

They lumbered toward her. Her face burned in the freezing wind. With each step, they were grosser, nastier, and the rotting stench like expired milk wafted heavier over Nikka. And with that, she couldn't help but feel there was another face below those horrific ones.

The beast on the right was almost within reach when she finally decided what to do.

The thing raised its six slick arms, and Nikka knew they would flatten her if she didn't act immediately. She watched its mouths crack open as it howled an ear-piercing screech, and she pointed her pistol right at the gap in the center of its face.

She fired three times. She couldn't take the chance of one bullet not being enough.

The monster stumbled and coughed out a dark-green substance. It slowed, and Nikka brightened with hope. It tumbled forward, and one of its massive, slimy arms grabbed Nikka and squeezed her.

The other beast blew past Nikka, and Lilly screamed and ran.

The first monster skidded on the trail, raising Nikka and pulling her close. It flopped on its stomach and dragged her toward its gnashing mouths.

"Let me go!" she screamed.

She didn't see where Lilly went, but she heard her howling in the forest.

The monster's mouths opened wide. Dark-green mucus sputtered from its openings. Teeth seemed to grow thicker and longer inside each maw as if the beast was getting aroused at the prospect of food. Its eyes stared her down, each of them feeling like it was piercing through her.

Nikka did the only thing she could think to do. She stuck the gun inside the monster's closest mouth, weaving her vulnerable flesh between its blade-like teeth, and pointed the barrel toward the center of the monster's head.

She pulled the trigger three more times.

Flames and smoke burst from each mouth. The sound drowned her ears in ringing and echoed into the forest.

At first, there was no change. She felt the creature's hot, rancid breath as her head was pulled closer and closer to its front-most mouth. She watched the opening widen even more. Then another wave of green slime erupted from the thing's jaws.

It shook, and it shook her. It squeezed her midsection, and the pressure in her head and down her sides made her think she was going to pop. Her eyes bulged and her ears swam. The gun went flying and her arms flailed. Then the thing went completely limp and dropped her on the forest floor, its slick arm still clinging around her waist.

"Fuck," she whimpered. Tears ran down her face. She could breathe. She fought to unwrap the thing's arm from her body, and below the putrid smell the creature effused in waves, Nikka recognized a scent that had been in her bed twice in the last few days. It wasn't a soap or shampoo or cologne. It was the scent he made below all that, the natural human aroma unique to each person, and this one was *his*.

She shivered as she looked once more up at the thing's misshapen skull. She told herself it couldn't have been true. There was no way that under this mutated flesh was someone she loved.

She cried. She couldn't stop herself from shaking.

It was insane. The thing before her was inhuman. It was demonic. But she couldn't shake the truth that she had just killed Mark for a second time.

Lilly's next howl was deep in the woods. It was cut short, and Nikka hated that she knew why.

Chapter Twenty-Four

THERE WAS A DISGUSTING stench on Nikka's clothes, and though she tried wiping it off as she hustled toward Rocky Bottom, the scent only seemed to smear on her fingers. The slickness left from the thing's arms lingered. It was a slimy reminder of what happened that hung in her mind and clung to her heart. It told her that there were rotten things ahead and that Masha would twist and corrupt anything Nikka cared for to kill her. It meant Nikka's success was not as assured as she had planned. It meant she needed to guard her heart as much as her body.

She was only one person now, no Lilly and no Mark. She had no more bullets. She was alone in the woods as she hurried toward Masha's shack, and she had only the will inside herself, an empty pistol, and the knife in her pack to do the job—or so she thought.

Still, she kept onward. There was no other choice. It seemed Masha wanted her dead as much as she wanted to kill the witch. She wondered if the monster that attacked Lilly was made from something close to Lilly as well. If those demons were from some kind of spell that required a connection or if Masha just used Mark because she was such a bitch.

Nikka pondered these things and wanted to stop and let herself wallow in the sorrow of everything she had lost. She hadn't had a moment to herself to think about Mark's death, and now that she was alone for the next steps, it all came crashing down on top of her like a lead blanket.

Each pace seemed harder than the last. Each breath was a struggle.

Her muscles and joints were all sore, and every movement was work—so much work just to keep going.

But she couldn't stop. The witch would be waiting. Night was coming. There was only forward. She needed to focus on the anger, the drive for revenge. That was the only way out of this. The dreams would surely come back no matter what, and in the end, that might drive her to something horrible, but with the witch gone, at least she would only have her own demons to battle. And the witch needed to pay.

The wind grew louder as Nikka found Rocky Bottom and started along the watery trail. The cracking boughs of tired branches echoed from near and far; the whistling of air racing through the needles above told of gusts that would fell a house, maybe even take a small one for a ride. It was like even the weather was holding her back, screaming for her to turn around—only she didn't know if it was a warning or a threat. Was it some benevolent force urging her away for her own safety? Or was it another of Masha's pawns trying to wear her down as she moved closer to the creek?

Nikka's face was numb when she reached the junction of Rocky Bottom and Black Creek. The tip of her nose and the rims of her ears were on fire with cold. There was a sour boiling inside her belly, and it crept up her throat toward her mouth, threatening to end the entire event before she set foot near the witch. It told her it could drag her to her knees the way Lilly had described the expulsion of her sickness, making her belly cramp so tight she wouldn't be able to move.

Nikka stared down the path ahead.

The light was thin. There was a hint of an orange glow from the west, behind the ridges, and narrow strips of blue clouds highlighted the atmosphere where the sky had already dedicated itself to night.

Her arrival was later than she had wanted. It would have been better to come during the daylight, but here she was. There had been no choice in the matter. Her instincts may have warned her that the witch was more dangerous at night, but Nikka was only so fast, and the forest had fought so hard to slow her down, and she couldn't have waited until dawn—not with the things that lived in those woods.

It was now or never.

With the knife in her hand, Nikka walked along the creek bed. There was a slithering sound in the muddy center, where not much more than a trickle of water flowed. Nikka wasn't surprised when she couldn't see the sound's cause. It was as devious as the noises from the woods, hiding their shapes, thriving on the fear they could induce. It was a game they were playing with Nikka, hoping to rattle her as she sought her goal—and it was working.

The spot where the shack should have been was a hundred feet away when the forest opened up and allowed Nikka to see. Instead of the shack that had welcomed her weeks ago, there was little more than a moldy pile of rotten logs. They made a square, tracing the shape of the ruined house, and a pile of stones that had once been a chimney lay strewn across the ground from the back of the debris into the tall weeds.

The sitting log was just as rotten. Large, wet, splintery gaps barely held the hunk of fibers together.

It was as if time and weather had been set in fast-forward and had taken the items that had been sitting there and eaten them away. Devoured them. Or had it all been a trick, an illusion that Masha had used to fool her?

And Nikka knew she was not alone.

She walked hesitantly toward the site, and as she moved, she felt the cold of the weather cutting her sharply, driving through her clothes like she was wearing nothing and chilling her deeper and deeper.

Masha was here, whether Nikka could see her or not. The evil was here. The power that directed her to follow Masha's tasks lived in this place and it was waiting for her.

She would wait too, wait for Masha to show her face.

Thunder rolled in from behind the woods. It wasn't like the noises back on the trail, though it wasn't like the noises in Nikka's dreams, either. There was something else coming, something she hadn't seen yet, and it was announcing its presence like the roar of an angry lion. It may have been hungry, but that wasn't what this was about. As a sound like a train crashed through the wall of trees ahead, as the wood shattered in a wave of splinters twenty feet wide, Nikka guarded her face and barely kept herself upright.

The forest fell to darkness, a thick, unnatural gloom that was almost impossible to see into. The moon was on the horizon, battling to rise over the eastern ridge, but it was too far and too faint to help Nikka. It was scenery, not illumination, and she strained to see what was coming. She wished she could be with Mom and Dad right then.

She last saw them on that dreamy beach. She would take that again. She would take spending another day with them in the dream house that was their old home. She would even take being with them in the afterlife, but that was her last resort. And that wasn't what they would have wanted. They would have wanted her to live her life, for her to see them in her dreams while succeeding and moving herself forward. They would want her to conquer this hurdle and go on to live her life.

Nikka imagined Mom and Dad watching her from above as the deafening sounds of whatever thing was approaching from the woods grew. She saw their eyes gazing at her with love and encouragement, and she stepped toward the witch's shack, clenching her fists: one ready to punch, one ready to stab.

Her hair whipped against the sides of her head as she neared the witch's house, and an amorphous shape breached the edge of the trees. The moon lifted over the mountain ridge, and through the dim blue light, she saw a thing of horror and awe.

She wanted to drop to her knees and beg it not to be real.

It barreled toward her on four things that could be construed as legs if it was actually a solid creature. Nikka wasn't sure if it was or wasn't. The flesh of its lower half seemed sometimes to be dark fog and sometimes murky liquid depending on how the light caught its features. Its arms were similar to the beast she had encountered before, with huge, flailing, snake-like things, but when it came to its shoulders and head—or heads—the similarities ended.

Above a pair of shoulders that were somewhere between a disgusting red jelly and a tangle of exposed muscle and organ was the thing's head. But it wasn't a single head. It was like someone had taken the heads of Lilly, Pastor Sanders, and Mark and smashed them into the flesh of a single being. Nikka clearly saw the process in her mind, the backs of their heads being cracked open and their brains being combined as their faces were sewn together into an abomination of death and depravity.

She fell to her knees at the fallen logs that marked the front of the shack. She hadn't imagined a thing as bad as this, and it froze her in place, her only movement the trembling of her hands.

The face of the holy man looked down on Nikka. Lilly stared blankly off to the side, as did Mark. Each face was pale and drooping like the skin was barely hanging on to the thing's giant head. Sanders's yellowed, bloodshot eyes met Nikka's, and a slow deranged smile crept across his dangling skin. His lips parted, and, for a second, Nikka thought he might speak, but what came out of his throat were the sounds of wailing. They were screams so loud they could have been from the halls of Hell itself. His teeth were broken into shattered points, and the inside of his mouth was black and dripping with blood.

This thing was not the pastor, at least not anymore. It was a thing, a monster; it only had the holy man's face.

And Mark's.

Mark's face was silent. It was so still that Nikka thought it was merely tacked on to horrify, until his eyes opened and searched. It wasn't the action of a man with all of his factors. It was the lazy scan of a mindless thing, a tortured thing stripped of its humanity and filled with agony and hate. Mark, whatever he had been, was no longer in that head.

Neither was Lilly.

She drooled blood, and her eyes bobbed as the creature walked. There was no one home inside her broken head.

Nikka gazed up at the atrocity and realized that all her bravado and courage up to that point meant nothing anymore. The horror before her drained her by its mere presence. The knife in her hand was meaningless if she didn't have the will to stand up and use it, if she couldn't force her body to overcome her fear and plunge it into that beast's belly.

The ground shook as it approached. The vibrations ran through her like waves of terror lapping over the shore. It was so near she could smell the death dripping from the monster's gelatinous limbs. She could smell the stench of the rotting faces on its head and the rancid breath as it heaved air over the clearing and down her throat.

It reached toward Nikka with a wide, lumbering swing. She felt the little warmth left in her body getting sucked away. She pictured it taking her into its arms and lifting her and ripping her face from her skull to add it to its collection. It was seconds away from stripping her flesh as it had the others, and she was helpless to rise and run, let alone rise and fight.

The chimney stones clattered under its limbs. The fallen logs splintered as it stormed over and crushed them. Its legs gripped the ground and slid like some kind of worm, but its arms were ready and willing to take her.

The limbs that wrapped around her were hard and slimy. The skin was elastic and rubbery but felt like the muscles of a bodybuilder beneath, and the stench made her head spin just from being near.

It lifted Nikka with one limb from each shoulder and held her up to the pastor's eyes. She could see its shifting yellow orbs were not veined with red as she first assumed. They were red with tiny swimming creatures, red worms or bugs or something. Urine ran down her legs as she imagined what this thing was going to do—how it planned to rip her head from her shoulders and use her face alongside the others. Would she be dead first and hopefully feel nothing? She wanted to puke.

It pulled her head toward the pastor's mouth, and out of nowhere, Nikka expelled a belt of screaming. She didn't know what it was. It was something primal inside that she had no control over. She howled like a bloodthirsty wolf.

She felt the monster's arms tightening around her. It was readying itself to squeeze her like a tube of toothpaste until her head popped. Then her arm acted on its own as well.

Her wrist turned, the blade flipping up, and with everything she had, she thrust her knife upward. It sank into the hard, rubbery surface of the monster's tentacle-like appendage, and the thing howled so loudly her head throbbed. It made her eardrums burn, and she wanted nothing more than to cover her ears and hide her head. But she couldn't reach. She could, however, pull back her blade, twisting it as it slid, and stab the giant creature yet again.

She rammed it deeper and felt liquid gush from the monster's wound. It ran over her wrist, and she twisted and stabbed again and again, until the monster bellowed so loudly that she thought she might become deaf. It made her pause and reassess, and she started again. She stabbed furiously, and this time, something different happened.

It raised Nikka over its heads, and she saw pure rage in its eyes and its distorted faces. It tossed her in disgust across the clearing, and she thudded then rolled into the center of the witch's ruined shack.

Nikka heard a thunk as the back of her head crashed into rotten wood. She fought to keep her eyes open. She was sure it would eat her if her eyes closed. But she couldn't stop her lids from falling.

205

Chapter Twenty-Five

THERE WAS A CRASH, and Nikka opened her eyes to her room, back in her family's home, back where everything started.

The crash repeated. It shook the bed. It shook her entire body. Pictures rattled on the walls and her lamp danced on her bedside table. There was a crackling sound from the outside wall between the crashes, and inside Nikka's mind, that crackling noise was a timer, a fuse burning itself down to—

Crash.

The window shattered inward, and a thousand razor-sharp crystals soared over Nikka's bed, along with splinters of wood and plaster. She closed her eyes tight, and they scraped her face as a boom that rocked the entire house resonated from her floor. And then another.

It felt instantaneous the way she opened her eyes, saw the monster halfway in her room and halfway out, and the way she rolled from bed and darted toward her door.

They were back. The giant bug-men were coming after her, and she was sure they were extra pissed after she had them banished for weeks. There were more coming up the side of the building; she could feel them getting closer. The one nearly inside her room was only the start. He was there to track her, to catch her and hold her in place so the rest could pick her apart.

It was all happening again.

She screamed as her foot was ripped open by glass and wooden splinters—not from the pain, but from the anger and frustration that this all felt inescapable. She had gotten away from it all but—

there's no such thing as a free lunch

—here she was again. That witch had given her a reprieve, but at the cost of her humanity, at the cost of walking on the edge of evil and being tempted to fall inside.

Nikka felt hot blood running from her soles as she yanked on the knob and her door flung open. She ran into the hallway and headed for the stairs.

The sound behind her was like a herd of horses stampeding through her bedroom and exploding through not just her door but through her wall and into the hall. She got a glimpse of its face as she turned and headed down the stairs. Its compound eyes bulged in balls of glossy blackness. Its mandibles were spread in anticipation of clamping into her flesh and holding her, ripping her, feeding her into its beak-like maw. Its enormous legs drove it forward with a supernatural speed, propelling it in a way that seemed only possible inside a dream, and—

Something struck Nikka, interrupting her thoughts as she raced down the stairs, focusing on each movement for speed and precision. She remembered all the psychologists she had seen, all the sleep therapists, all the books and websites and videos she had watched—all of them had tried to treat her mind from the outside. They had all dealt with trying to fix her mind while she was awake. She wondered if somehow the solution was not to fix herself from out there, but from in here.

When she had first met Masha, it was inside her dreams, and Masha somehow got into her mind and changed things to suit her needs and comfort Nikka. Nikka wondered if she was able to do that for herself. It was *her* mind, after all. It was her brain allowing these things to happen, wasn't it?

She set foot on the bottom step and raised her gaze to see three things: she saw Mom and Dad in the center of the room, and her heart was at once relieved at being near them and terrified for their safety; she saw the windows to the outside world and bug-men raising their tree-trunk-sized legs to break through; and she saw Masha in the dark and distant corner of the room.

"Nikka!" Mom raised her arms to embrace her child as soon as she saw her. Her face was textured in wrinkles of fear.

Dad's mouth hung open as he stared at the window and the black legs smashing through.

"Mom!" Nikka ran and wrapped her arms around her mother.

The beast from upstairs crashed over the last few steps and hovered in the entrance to the living room. The two living room windows burst as two more bug-men came through each. They surrounded Nikka and her parents, and a high cackle rose from the corner.

The monstrous beasts' feet made a rumble that traveled up Nikka's spine as they closed in, and the entire room seemed to shrink. Nikka held Mom and Dad, and they clutched her tightly. The stink of dank earth and mold was heavy in the air, and as Nikka flexed her grip on her mother and father, she tried hard to devise a plan.

For once in a long time, she didn't accept the rule that the past years had taught her, that she was doomed and these things would claw and tear her apart. If the witch had been able to change her dreams for the better, so could she. They were *her* dreams. This was *her* head.

Thoughts of every moment, every joyful second Nikka had spent with her family, ran through her mind. One stuck out, one that was laughs and excitement, exhilaration. She focused hard on that moment in the past, when Dad grinned from ear to ear and the warmth of Mom's touch hung in her memory like a gleaming lighthouse to signal Nikka.

She squeezed her eyes closed and ignored the thundering footfalls of monsters. She ignored the rhythmic cackling of the witch. She held tighter to Mom and Dad, and a second later, all the noise stopped.

She was somewhere else.

Nikka opened her eyes to a bright sunny day. She heard the rumble of wheels on metal tracks and smelled popcorn, cotton candy, and funnel cakes. There was a crowd of people going from shop to shop and ride to ride. She was at the carnival, holding Mom's hand in one of hers and Dad's in the other.

"Nikka?" Mom asked. She was scanning the crowd. Her face didn't have the joy Nikka remembered from their last trip to the carnival; it was worried.

"How did we get here?" Dad asked.

"I think I brought us here," Nikka said. She searched the crowds and saw families. She saw moms with kids and teenagers. She saw men in cowboy hats who had obviously been at the rodeo that was held on that same weekend every year.

She wanted to smile. They had escaped the house and the monsters and Masha, but something told her it wasn't enough.

One scream overtook the joyous sounds of amusement riders. It was harsh and pained, and a half second later, others joined it.

Nikka spun.

The crowd split as screams grew. There was a bug-man impaling a carnival-goer between its legs as it ripped the human in two. It flung the bisected man to one side, and a wave of blood and viscera splashed people as they ran.

"It's back," Dad shouted.

More screams came from behind them, more from the side. The monsters had appeared in the middle of the crowd and were smashing and stomping on people all around Nikka. And they were coming closer.

The cackling returned. It was higher pitched. Masha was laughing through the voice of an old woman, dried up and unrelenting.

"No!" Nikka pulled her family in closer. "No."

How could this be happening? She had taken her parents away from their home. This was a different place and time. It was a place she had resurrected from her memories. How could they have followed them?

And she understood. She may have run, but she didn't defeat them. She was still inside her head, and so was Masha. If she wanted to get away, she couldn't just run. She had to destroy them.

Screams got louder and blood sprayed inside the frantic crowd. Nikka held Mom's and Dad's hands tightly and ran, dragging them along.

They cut right, around the Gravitron and she pulled Mom and Dad into the gated area where the Ferris wheel stood. She backed up slowly under the giant wheel as the bug-men climbed the fence and headed straight for them.

Nikka could feel their glares and their hatred. They wanted to taste her, and they were furious she had gotten away from them.

She kept backing away. She stepped out from under the wheel, and the three monsters stepped below it.

Nikka didn't know if this was going to work, but she knew it *had* to. It was her first time trying something like this, but she had transported them there—she had to have the power to make this happen.

She closed her eyes and pictured what she wanted. She squeezed Mom's and Dad's hands. They gave her strength. She knew they weren't the real Mom and Dad, just a dream version of them, but here, they were the next best thing, and she used that to empower herself.

There was a crunching, metallic sound, a whine and crack, and Nikka opened her eyes to see if what she wished had come true.

She pulled her parents back, and a mass of welded and riveted steel came crashing down. The entire Ferris wheel smashed into the ground in a rusted web of metal that landed directly on the three abominations.

Corroded blue steel crushed through chitinous exoskeletons. Thick bug legs snapped, and a sea of goo and strand-like muscle ruptured from their openings like fountains. Bug heads exploded under the pressure, and mandibles, eyes, and thick, spiny hair burst as the wheel continued to collapse, break over itself, and stack metal into a giant pile of jagged, rusty beams.

The noise was ear-piercing. The squeak and crunch of metal, the bassy boom of the ground, it consumed all, and Nikka was deaf to everything else until the wheel finished falling and her back was against the fence.

Then the witch's laughter returned.

The bright light faded from the sky, and darkness covered the fairgrounds. The last scream of a fairgoer faded, and Nikka knew they were there alone. Alone with the witch.

"Come on." Nikka urged her parents forward. They climbed the fence and ran into the next row of attractions.

The witch was even louder.

Mom and Dad ran, looking for her.

They didn't see Masha, but she was unavoidable. She was inside Nikka's head as much as Nikka was in her own, and she didn't think the same kind of trick that killed the bugs would work on the witch. But she had to try something.

Nikka saw the sign for the funhouse. She pulled Mom and Dad there, and they stood at its entrance, waiting.

"Show yourself, Masha!" she screamed into the dark carnival.

It was like they were in the middle of an apocalypse. The amusements were cold and silent, strange in their darkness. Not a bulb was lit. Not a car or game or generator stirred. There were no stars above as if the suns had been extinguished or a blanket had been pulled over the night.

"Where are you, Masha?" Nikka called. "The deal is over. Dead. No more tasks. I'll handle my dreams myself, and you can keep your weird cannibal bullshit to yourself."

As soon as the words left her mouth, she knew it was harder than that. She couldn't just quit after letting the witch into her soul even if it did sound like she was negotiating for peace. Her stomach wanted more Lucky Shot Burgers. She craved them the second she thought about them. She knew that if she were at home again, or on that beach, she would happily raise one to her lips and take a bite, and—a thought crossed her mind, a trick that might just have a chance.

She held Mom's and Dad's hands tightly and concentrated once more.

"Come on, you bitch!"

There was a sound like whooshing, and Nikka's ears popped. She saw sunlight through her closed lids, and she knew they had been transported again. The sea crashed on the beach, and the smell of salt was in her nose. Then there was the whirring mechanical noise of a plane's jet engine.

She opened her eyes and saw a South Pacific beach. Chunks of plane wreckage were all over the dunes, and a single spinning engine was ahead, sucking in the air, lost and unaware that it was no longer flying high over the Pacific.

"Nikka?" Mom asked. "What's going on?"

"This... This is from a TV show," Dad said.

Only a second passed before the witch's laugh was in Nikka's head. She turned and saw Masha.

She was slender with long hair that danced in the tropical wind. She was young, and she marched toward Nikka with a smirk on her face, her white dress clinging to her body in front, fluttering in the wind behind her.

"Talk to me, Masha," Nikka said. "We can work this out."

Masha moved closer; she was maybe twenty feet away. She had no weapon in her hands—she carried nothing—but Nikka knew the witch didn't need a thing to end this all with everyone covered in blood.

She spoke, and it echoed in Nikka's head. "You had your chance. We had a deal, and you broke it. Now, everything you are is mine."

Nikka ushered her parents behind her, and they stepped to the side, the opposite side of the roaring engine as Masha.

"We don't have to do this, Masha!" Nikka shouted over the engine. "We can just go our separate ways!"

Keep moving closer, Nikka called inside her mind. *Keep following.*

Masha came. Her expression was playful, a smirk, a hunter toying with its prey. The witch stepped in front of the engine, and Nikka held her mother's and father's hands even tighter. She focused on the sound, the loud revving that sucked in air and thrust it back toward the sea. She wished and then commanded, and the engine was suddenly louder, the suction stronger, and Masha's clothes whipped toward the spinning mechanism. Her hair shot from her head toward it, and she started sliding in the sand in the direction of the massive intake. Masha looked curiously at the machine, and it revved even louder. Nikka gritted her teeth, watching, forcing it to be stronger and faster.

The witch let out the start of a chuckle and was ripped from the ground and sucked toward the device.

Nikka's heart skipped a beat as she watched the witch fly through the air. She had won. She had tricked the witch and saved herself and her parents. She had—

Nikka turned cold, and the entire beach seemed to freeze. There was no more wind and no more waves. The engine went silent, and the witch floated just in front of her disassembly. She continued her chuckle and floated toward Nikka.

"No!" Nikka shouted. She willed harder, trying to get the engine spinning again. It had to work. She had to kill the witch.

"I like this thing." Masha pointed at the jet engine. She floated closer and set foot on the ground just a few feet from Nikka. "I want to see it work."

She stared at Nikka, through Nikka, and the world came back to life. The engine screamed, this time hungrily, and without so much as a blink, the witch made it happen.

Mom and Dad shot from the ground, propelled like bullets toward the spinning mechanism.

Nikka started to scream, but before her words left her mouth, her parents were fed head-first into the whirring blades. A cloud of red mist went flying out the back. Only a scarlet stain remained on the screaming aircraft components, and Mom and Dad were gone, devoured by a supercharged blender into nothingness.

Nikka's scream came out as a wall. It slammed into Masha, throwing the witch backward and shaking the world in an earthquake that cracked open the beach and made the ocean waves rush backward. Trees toppled, and the sun vibrated.

She screamed again, and it was even louder. It was sorrow, and it was rage. It was the past two years' worth of mourning and anger in a single outward breath.

Masha's face lost its smile.

The sun went black, and as if unable to contain Nikka's call, the entire world exploded.

Chapter Twenty-Six

L IKE SO MANY TIMES over the past two years, Nikka woke to the sound of her own screaming.

Night had fully enclosed the clearing where she lay in the middle of the ruins of Masha's shack. The moon cast soft, blue light over the aged remains, the rotten logs that had once been walls, and the forest around.

Nikka blinked with heavy eyes as she saw this place for once as it really was, unhindered by the mask the witch had laid over it every time before. The trees were cracked and skeletal, frames of old trunks that had withered over time to eerie bones. The ground was nearly barren with black, oily mud. The stream was a scar of oil-drenched rock, rubble, and mud that couldn't have held life in the last hundred years. The entire area was a place of waste as if something had drained the life away until there was nothing, leaving only the sludge of death across each surface. Even the magpies and crows that now perched on the trees and watched were things of death, degraded and mangled, dripping with the evil sludge that seemed to own everything in sight.

The beast with three faces stood outside the boundary of the witch's home. It panted and heaved up and down as it breathed in massive gusts. It stared at Nikka with all three sets of eyes, its teeth grinding, yet it didn't dare break the plane that had once been *her* walls.

Nikka's head ached. She cupped the back of her skull as she climbed to her feet. She remembered every bit of her dream, every fear, every tear, and every ounce of anger. She looked around for Masha, knowing this wasn't over, and she looked the beast up and down, questioning her next move.

She gripped her knife's handle and screamed in no particular direction, "Come out, Masha! Quit hiding behind your monsters! I know you're not scared of a little girl with bad dreams!"

A harsh wind blew from above, and the chill froze Nikka to her bones. There were yips and screams from the woods. Black eyes blinked from the darkness.

The three-faced monster howled and vibrated, and it melted in front of Nikka. Its legs dissolved first, then its arms. Its faces, the faces of people she knew, were the most horrific to watch. Skin liquefied, turning to blood and running down into the earth as their faces contorted in anguish, screaming, their muscles and bones becoming nothing more than a puddle, and their remains pooled over the sopping soil.

The ground rumbled, and the sky faded into complete darkness. The trees fell away from view, and only the ground under Masha's shack remained. It was like the lights of the world had been extinguished and a single spotlight fell on the square where she stood.

Then Masha came into view, only it was the oldest version of Masha Nikka had seen. Thin, broken skin hung from her face with open wounds that pussed and ran with infection. The few teeth she had were rotten and yellow with black spots. White, patchy hair sprung from her narrow skull. Her clothes were ratty and torn, barely held together by strands, and her gait was limping and awkward as she approached. But the worst part of her appearance was her eyes. They were more like black holes in her skull that held cavernous dark. They were like a door to a demonic world, and all that came out was a line of sludge that walked down her cheeks in an oily streak.

She was more dead than alive, more evil and inhuman than a person.

She stared at Nikka through those orbless eyes, and that was when Nikka noticed her hand and her necklace.

The rope around Masha's neck was decorated with a dozen desiccated fingers. They were bone and dried-up skin and nothing more, yet Nikka could tell Masha wore them with pride, with power.

Masha's hand, though, that was missing four fingers. Ragged stumps bulged from her knuckles. They were open, festering wounds, puss-filled and wet, like they were severed years ago but never allowed to heal.

Nikka saw these disgusting images, and it suddenly became clear exactly what she had to do.

The witch was fifteen feet away and closing. Nikka didn't have much time. She dropped to her knees and let her backpack slide around to her front. She reached into a large pocket and didn't find what she was looking for, so she dug into the next one.

Panic set in—it wasn't there either.

She checked the next one, her fingers moving quickly, then frantically. The witch was getting closer and she still hadn't found—

There it was, a cold plastic bag.

She ripped it from the backpack and held it high, and as she did, Masha's mouth dropped open. Animals screeched and howled in the woods, and Nikka saw them in her mind, skinny vessels of death, not much more than furry bags of bones.

They saw what Masha saw.

Nikka reached back into her bag and grabbed a pair of gloves, another item which, like the bag of fingers she had received from the freaks in Custer Falls, was something she hadn't known why she had brought—until now. Both were the result of her gut demanding it.

"Those are mine!" Masha screamed as she hobbled faster toward her shack.

Nikka opened the base of the left glove and slid one finger into each of the four long slots. Then she placed her left hand on the closest log.

"You bitch!" Masha screamed.

Nikka lowered her knife over the knuckle that attached her index finger to her left hand. She felt a wave of fear pass over her. What if this was the wrong choice? What if she was disfiguring herself for no reason and she would be forced to live with this for the rest of her life?

There is no rest of my life *if this doesn't work*, she told herself.

She shoved the blade through her flesh, slicing skin then tendon, and scraping past bone. The finger—her finger, the thing that had been a part of her her entire life and never would be again—rolled off the log and onto the oily dirt.

The pain was hot and instantaneous, but she had no time to acknowledge it.

Nikka lined up the next two fingers together and pressed down with all her might. The blade sank into her middle finger and was halfway through, but it caught on the bone of her ring finger, snagging just under the skin and inside the tendons.

It hurt worse than anything in her entire life. Worse than her worst period, worse than the cavity she hid from her parents for six months when she was nine because she didn't want to go to the dentist, worse than when she broke her arm skiing in the fifth grade.

It made her stomach clench tight, ready to spew, and her vision waved like hot air over a scorching road.

She pulled out the knife. She had no choice.

Nikka sliced quickly into her middle finger, finishing the cut, and she started the ring finger over again. Both digits rolled into the mud, and she dared a look at Masha.

The witch's face was a ball of demonic anger. She was three feet away and reaching, extending her clawed right hand toward Nikka.

"Mine!" Masha screamed.

Nikka rushed to line up her knife with her pinkie. She only had a moment. She pressed through skin and tendon, gliding through the gap between the bones of her knuckle, and Masha's clawed hand grabbed her hair and jerked her head to the side.

Nikka screamed. She fell backward with Masha. The hand on her head felt like the rocky hand of a stone monster. The old woman's strength was like a gorilla, the way she tossed Nikka to one side. She slammed into the earth, and Masha was on top of her, her jaws spreading and the tips of small, jagged teeth rising through her gums.

What is she?

Nikka did the only thing she could think of. She thrust her knife upward into Masha's chest. It ran through paper-thin skin, and there was a popping sound as it punctured her lung. Nikka twisted the blade and shoved it around and right, jabbing into where she was sure Masha's heart should have been.

Masha howled and jumped back. She was like an animal the way she moved, and the creatures in the woods and in the trees called through the night. Their voices were hollow yet angry. They wanted to see blood. They wanted death.

Nikka looked down at her hands. The cutting wasn't done. Her finger dangled from her hand with only a small strand of flesh keeping it attached, and Masha had jumped away with the knife.

She stared at Masha, and the world around them narrowed. The sky and the blackness closed in like a shrinking ebony box. There was more on the other side of those unseen walls, and Nikka could feel it. There was another place beyond the cold gloom, a place of angry souls and demons. It was the place on the other side of the fog, on the other side of those oily walls. It was a bustling residence of evil, and the borders were shrinking around her.

The old woman's legs stretched, and she grew taller. Her arms extended, almost looking like she was melting, and then her face darkened and lengthened, and her shape turned into something resembling a demonic elf. She grabbed the blade in her chest with her good hand, ripped it free, and tossed it to the side.

Eyes appeared in Masha's face, but not the eyes of a human. They were solid red, and they looked back at Nikka with a ferocious glare as the old witch began sweating black slime from every inch of her skin.

There was no time for Nikka to do anything other than what she had to. She seized the mostly dismembered finger in her right hand and screamed as she ripped it from her knuckle. She grabbed the glove she had shoved the others' fingers inside and dragged it over her bleeding hand.

Masha leaped again, her jaws spreading, her new fangs long and hungering, and she came down over Nikka.

Nikka felt her blood filling the glove. Even with her severed nerves, she felt the mortician's, the butcher's, the pastor's, and the fast-food manager's fingers next to her wounds. But more than that, as her blood seeped into their flesh, she could sense what could only be her stumps joining them. It started as a wash of pain and phantom sensations, but as her blood soaked those fingers, hydrated them, slipped under the skin, it was like her life was giving them new life. It was like they were joining her, and those phantom sensations turned into real ones at the tips of her new appendages. And more than that, it was like their lives, their souls, were sending strength up through her hand and into her body, into her mind.

Suddenly, Nikka saw through Masha's facade. She didn't see a witch coming down on her. She saw a monster, a demon in an old witch's flesh, looking for the souls of men to refill its power lost through age. It was a demon from Hell that had infested the witch's body long ago and was seeking new power from the residents of Custer Falls. It was taking from the murdered and eaten, taking from those tricked into cannibalism, and it wanted Nikka to die and get out of the way.

Nikka jerked to the side, and the demon chomped down on oily mud. She pushed herself up and jumped from inside the shack. The demon hopped onto all fours and charged.

Nikka didn't understand what happened next; she just let go and followed her instincts.

The old demon reached again, leaped again, and Nikka ducked but let her gloved hand reach forward, grabbing the demon's necklace of fingers and ripping it hard from the monster's neck.

The necklace snapped.

The Masha-demon howled. It melted, shedding skin and muscle, its head waving left and right as streams of flesh were strewn across the ground, until the thing was again the size of the old woman. But Nikka didn't stay still to watch it happen. She traded the necklace from one hand to the other, and she wrapped it around the glove as she ran.

There was a galloping sound behind Nikka, and she knew she only had a second. Her eyes scanned the ground as she prayed, looking for the smallest sign, the slightest glint.

There was no moon, but the ambiance showed her a sliver of light shining in the dirt. She lunged for it and reached with her gloved hand.

The old demon landed on Nikka's back. She felt it latch on like a rodeo rider, clamping down around her hips and shoulders.

Nikka clutched her knife's handle in her gloved hand, and she felt fangs sink into her shoulder. They were cold, so cold they burned her insides from there to her lungs, and the pain was electrifying. It demanded she close her eyes. She couldn't see, and the world was a wall of white.

Again she let her gut guide her.

She spun, and with only hope on her side, Nikka stabbed blindly.

There was a screeching howl, a scream so loud it blocked out everything else. There was brightness; a thing happened that shined through her closed lids and let her see it all.

Her gloved hand was the catalyst. Each finger shared its power and lit the string around her hand like a strand of finger-shaped Christmas lights. The fingers inside her glove were glowing. They wrapped around the handle and made the blade shine. The steel dove deep inside the monster's heart, and the organ pumped a slow, soiled beat—a cantankerous effort, trying its hardest to refuse. Then the beast erupted—exploded in a ball of reddish gore that took the demon's entire body and splattered it across the clearing into a thousand unrecognizable chunks.

It took a minute before Nikka could see again. When her sight returned, the moon was back. The clearing was barren of gore, and in its place were the tiniest blades of grass. The oily mud was gone. The slime over stone and trees had vanished. The ruins of the shack were gone, and the stream ran with a clear steady flow.

It made her laugh, until she pulled off the glove.

The four fingers were no longer fused to her hand like they had felt inside that glove. Instead, there were four healed stumps—healed so thoroughly they looked like a surgeon had taken her digits years ago.

She looked around. She looked down. She cried. It wasn't because her fingers were gone; she could live with that. It was because for the first time in her life, she was finally in charge. She wouldn't be bossed around by the witch or commanded by a parent. She wouldn't be ruled over by her dreams or lack of sleep. She would rule over them. She felt the strength inside herself just like the way she had commanded her dreams to react.

She cried because this wasn't the end she had thought it would surely be. This was truly her beginning.

Epilogue

In the months that followed Nikka's trips into the woods, anonymous phone calls tipped off the police to strange goings-on at the mortuary, the butcher shop, the church, and the burger joint. Unfortunately, the cops didn't find anything actionable, and no one was arrested. The mortuary had been cleaned of its bodies as if something had warned Ramon trouble was coming. The butcher shop had no human meat in its freezers. The church was thriving with dozens of happy parishioner witnesses. And the burger joint passed their Health Department inspection with flying colors. It was like they had made deals for their souls.

Fortunately, Nikka's cravings for Lucky Shot Burger went away, and she hadn't set foot inside one since—or had them delivered.

Inside Lilly's apartment was another story. As soon as the witch died, every resident in Custer Falls seemed to instantly smell the decomposition in her apartment. Over the course of the weeks following Nikka's return home, arrest warrants were issued for Lilly for suspicion in the deaths of dozens of people, including Mark, his brother, Adrian, Rich, Lynn, a missing preacher, and many more. They put out APBs, and everyone in town was on the lookout for her. They would all be disappointed when she never returned to face justice.

Nikka held tight to her plans. She finished her online courses and over the summer moved to Alaska, enrolling in the University of Alaska for the following semester.

There were no Lucky Shot Burgers in Anchorage.

Her dreams from then on weren't perfect, but they were better. She was confident more often, and the bug-men, when they showed up, met their match. She saw her parents and enjoyed their company even though their faces were starting to get blurry as time passed and she needed them less and less. It wasn't something she liked, but it was something she accepted.

Occasionally, Nikka found herself awake and thinking of Mom and Dad and the special times, the hotels and the jokes on the long car rides that made her laugh for hours. When she thought of those, she remembered them perfectly clearly. She allowed the rest to fade because it let her make sure it was the real memories she was treasuring and not the ones she dreamed up—definitely not the ones where monsters ripped them apart and not the ones where they were sucked into a jet engine. She had to keep it all sorted out, and letting some of the memories go was part of that.

In her second semester at UA, while the wind whipped outside and the temps were negative daily, Nikka met another student, named Justin, who swept her off her feet. They were inseparable from then on. He didn't mind her missing fingers or her occasional night terrors. He stood by her as she held true to her decision to graduate and make her lost parents proud.

Justin never asked Nikka about the glove filled with four fingers he stumbled upon in her freezer one day, and he never tried to make her eat burgers, which she was staunchly against. When he started getting emails from a website about the legend of a witch in the Alaskan bush, he didn't even mention it to her, knowing her hatred for anything having to do with witchcraft.

He went to check that out himself, not knowing that she would follow him, not knowing that some witches were better left as legends.

225

Acknowledgements

Black Creek Mystic was a lot of work, through long nights and weekends. It would not exist without the effort and kindness of many people. I thank you all and regret those I may have missed. This is just a token.

Christina Hitz — Thank you for sacrificing time together, encouraging me, and picking up all the pieces I missed through my absent-mindedness. Thank you for encouraging me and being there when I needed you.

My kids — Thank you for believing in me and giving me the space I needed to work, especially when you wanted to write your own words into the pages.

Melinda Parrish — Thank you for reading my work over the years, believing in me, and pushing me to put it out there.

My Editor: **Heather Ann Larson**, your keen eyes and attention to detail really helped to pull this book together. Thank you.

My Cover Designer: **Don Noble**, your art brought this thing to life for readers. Keep strutting that massive talent.

My Patreon members: Thank you for your support along this journey. It was a blast writing as you read. Special thanks to **Jay Bower** and **Jordan Triplett**.

About the Author

D.W. Hitz loves the outdoors and enjoys making it a background character in his work. He devours stories in all mediums. He enjoys writing in the genres of Horror, Supernatural/Paranormal Thriller, and Science Fiction/Fantasy. He aspires to tell stories that thrill the heart and stimulate the imagination.

When not writing, D.W. enjoys spending time with his family, hiking, camping, and playing with the dogs.

———————————

Stay up to date with D.W. by becoming a member at
patreon.com/dwhitz

What's Next?

Check out more horror by D.W. Hitz and Fedowar Press.

Garrets Lodge by D.W. Hitz

Something is stirring in the woods outside Custer Falls. A haunted place that's been waiting a very long time.

Wanda heads out on a hike with friends. Stevie and Honey flee into the woods from the cops. They all think the woods will be their salvation until they find the terrors at Garrets Lodge.

Our Trip Through Hell by D.W. Hitz

Missy was always forbidden from visiting the abandoned cemetery. She listened for most of her life, but now her father's tales of buried gold and family treasure are proving too tempting for her and her friends to resist.

On a cold November night, it becomes a portal to Hell. If they want to return, they'll have to fight for it.

Camp Slasher Lake: Volume 3

A tribute to the glorious slasher movies of the 1980s, Volume 3.

Featuring stories by Jonathan Maberry, Will Suffer, MJ Mars, Brian G. Berry, Megan Stockton, Jay Bower, Eric Butler, M Ennenbach, RJ Roles, Angel Van Atta, and D.W. Hitz

Uncanny Valley Days by C.J. Sampera

Rocked by grief and recurring apparitions of her dead brother, Olivia is losing her grip on reality and may have inadvertently invoked a cybernetic, serial-killing slasher demon. Or is it all in her head?

Bloodtooth by D.W. Hitz

After nightmares begin in the small town of Custer Falls, Montana, in 1992, it'll be thirty years before they end.

After Wes Henson and his friends' field trip to Bloodtooth Caverns, everything changes. All they did was stray off the path. They didn't expect to break their bones and discover an ancient relic. But once it's in Wes's hands, he's the one that has to put it back. Because when this evil is awake, no one's dreams are safe.

Thank You for
Reading